When the Green
GRASS
GROWS

When the Green
GRASS
GROWS

GROWING UP IN
Detroit

SHIRLEY BERGSTROM

TATE PUBLISHING
AND ENTERPRISES, LLC

Published by Tate Publishing & Enterprises, LLC
127 E. Trade Center Terrace | Mustang, Oklahoma 73064 USA
1.888.361.9473 | www.tatepublishing.com

Tate Publishing is committed to excellence in the publishing industry. The company reflects the philosophy established by the founders, based on Psalm 68:11,
"The Lord gave the word and great was the company of those who published it."

Book design copyright © 2015 by Tate Publishing, LLC. All rights reserved.
Cover design by Samson Lim
Interior design by Mary Jean Archival

Published in the United States of America

ISBN: 978-1-68237-306-4
Fiction / Family Life
15.09.18

This novel is about growing up in Detroit when the city became the Motor Capital of the world. What was it like living in this city where jobs were abundant and cars were shipped to every continent in the world? People migrated to Detroit from most every state in the Union. There was always somewhere to go, something new and fresh that one could do. It became a thriving metropolis where you could buy most anything available. Living in this city during the Depression and World War II saw a lot of changes. I remember gas rationing and sugar rationing, blackouts, air raid sirens blasting away. Jobs were lost during the Depression. I lived there through thick and thin. I remember the war songs and people enlisting in one branch of the service or another. These times were indelibly etched in my brain. I shall never forget them. I grew up on the west side of Detroit. Let me relive my childhood to you through this book. On July 7, 1947, I watched the entourage of Henry Ford's funeral as it made its way to the cemetery of Saint Martha's Episcopal Church. I stood on the corner of Greenfield and Joy Road as he was laid to rest. Most people believe he was laid to rest in Dearborn, but I knew it was Detroit. I was there. I witnessed it. Read this book and find out the rest of the story of how it was like to be raised in Detroit, Michigan.

1

Once upon a time in the Scandinavian country of Sweden, two young people met and fell in love. The name of the village was Bör Jo, on a farm called a croft. They worked for a wealthy landowner named Gustaf Olaf Romblom. Famine was sweeping across the land. No land was available for a family to purchase. Most of Sweden was owned by wealthy landowners called crofters. They would hire the common folks to come and farm their land.

It was during the late 1800s that about one quarter of the Swedish population migrated to the United States to escape the famine and destitution of Swedish life. They had heard of land available and all kinds of opportunities to fulfill their dreams.

Sven Stordahl and Gertrude Peterson were married in the ancient cathedral in Bör Jo. They planned to start their married life by relocating to the United States of America. They both had been saving for several years to make this daring move.

The day had finally arrived when they boarded the big ship that would take them to the new land. It was a long, arduous journey. Some days the seas were rough. It was about a three-week sail from Stockholm to Ellis Island in New York. When they saw the Statute of Liberty, their hearts pounded within them in anxious anticipation.

They had relatives that had made their way to Cheboygan, Michigan, to become employed at a sawmill in Duncan City, a neighboring village. Relatives who lived there wrote letters to them, telling of this place they would now call home. These relatives lived three miles from Duncan City in a place called Swede Town, not far from the shores of Lake Huron. They arrived in June of 1886. Gertrude was six months pregnant at the time.

When they arrived at Swede Town, their relatives and friends greeted them, took them in, and fed them until their home could be built on Butler Street.

It came to pass that they were deeded a twenty-acre plot of land from the Land Office. All they had to do was live there for seven years and then the land would be theirs. This was because of the Homestead Act of 1862, which had been signed by President Abraham Lincoln. Anyone who had not taken up arms against the United States and were twenty-one years of age could apply for land. No money was involved, just occupy the land, build a house, and maybe raise crops.

In 1887, a church was built next to the Swedish schoolhouse. Olaf Romblom operated a store from their home where the settlers could buy staples.

Sven and Gertrude became parents of Eric Olaf on January 1, 1887. Olaf Romblom employed Sven at his lumber camp four miles from Swede Town. Little Eric was baptized when he was two weeks old by Rev. P. O. Lindman. He was a fair-haired little Swede who looked like his father. He was joined in years to come by four brothers and three sisters.

Sven only worked at the lumber camp for two years, and then he worked to develop his farm into a thriving rural homestead. He grew cucumbers for a pickling factory. He raised cattle for beef. He grew his own hay for feed and sold butter, eggs, and cream to the local farmers. Little Eric, because he was the oldest, helped his father and did chores out on the farm. As the oldest son, he was more dependable, not afraid of hard work and laboring in the hot summer sun.

When Eric was eighteen, he decided to move to Detroit to get a job working in a garage that repaired automobiles. He was a very handsome young man with ash blonde hair, blue eyes, and a jovial, fun-loving disposition. He was about five foot ten inches tall. He was a lot of fun to be with. He was very muscular from working on the farm. In many ways, he was just like his father. His father, who loved him dearly, missed his help on the farm. Many of the young people from Swede Town, gals and guys alike, wanted to go where jobs were plentiful, and so they also made their way to the big City of Detroit. On Sundays, they made their way to the Evangelical Swedish Mission Church in Detroit on Fourteenth and Antoinette. Here, Eric met the daughter of Mrs. Murphy. Her name was Colleen, and in time to come, they fell in love, and in September of 1925, they were married at the Mission Church.

They honeymooned in Cheboygan and stayed at the Stordahl homestead. Sven and Gertrude loved Colleen, even though she was not Swedish. Returning back to Detroit, they rented a home at 1932 Steel Street. They lived in the upstairs flat of the two-story house.

When you entered through the door, there was a hall and staircase. The staircase led to the upper flat. A door opened to the kitchen and left was the opening to the dining room with the living room on the right. At the right, a hallway led to two bedrooms and the bathroom. The larger bedroom had a porch on it where you could look into the lot in back where a peach tree grew. These were very tasty peaches.

Colleen continued working for her mother at the boarding house. She rode with Eric every day as the boarding house was not very far from the job where he was employed. She was an Irish lassie with red hair, a few freckles, and quite a pretty girl. She loved Eric dearly and they made a charming couple.

They had only been back in Detroit a few days from their honeymoon when Eric received a telegram:

ERIC, YOUR MOTHER AND FATHER WERE KILLED IN A HOUSE FIRE. RETURN TO CHEBOYGAN—HANS STORDAHL.

When Eric received the wire, he immediately left for Cheboygan. Colleen stayed at home as her mother needed her help. Eric stayed at his brother's house. All the rest of the siblings had also gone to the Motor City, and they, too, headed back to their old homestead only to see that there was nothing left but a pile of ashes. They were told that it was a chimney fire, and the roof burned quickly and spread to the rest of the house.

The residents of Swede Town grieved with the family, for this couple who had endeared themselves in the lives of those immigrants. The house fire made headlines in the *Cheboygan Daily Tribune* with a picture of Sven and Gertrude on the front page. It was a somber gathering at the Swedish Church in Swede Town. Rev. P. O. Lindman officiated at the funeral, which was all preached in Swedish.

The sawmill at Duncan City had burned down in the late 1800s, so Swede Town was now part of Cheboygan, Michigan. Duncan City was no more.

Eric and his siblings sat side by side and still couldn't believe their parents were gone. Sven and Gertrude Stordahl were in their early sixties when the fire took place.

It was a long dismal ride back home to Detroit. All the family attended the Swedish church in Detroit. Eric's brother, Emanuel, taught the men's Bible class. Ruth, his younger sister, taught the women's Bible class. Judith played the piano. Elmer and Andrew became ushers and Esther taught Sunday school.

2

In the weeks to come, Eric thought of his life growing up on the farm. His dad, Sven, had a hard time expressing the word *spring* in English. His favorite saying was, "When the green grass grows, I will do such and such," mainly planting his gardens, which were a source of income for the family during the harvest time.

So it was with Eric. He would say that phrase often in years to come concerning future events for his family.

In January, Colleen found herself pregnant with their first child, who would be born sometime in August. And so it was, on August 19, 1926, Dr. Ross B. Richardson was called to the home on Steel to deliver their firstborn child.

The baby weighed seven and a half pounds, but only lived a few hours. She was a blue baby. Heart problems ran in some of Eric's relatives, and this little one was one of them. Eric's grandfather had died of a massive heart attack when he was just fifty years old.

Colleen wept for days on end. The tiny infant was laid to rest at Evergreen Cemetery. So for the next few years, "when the green grass grows," they would go and plant flowers on her grave.

In 1931, Eric lost his job at the garage. The country was in the throes of a Great Depression. In June of that year, Colleen was once again pregnant. Because the economy was so bad and with Eric out of a job, the young couple found themselves wondering what to do. No money meant they could no longer afford their rent. Eric knew farming and could help out the folks back in Cheboygan, so they moved back to Cheboygan and stayed with Hans, waiting for the Depression to end and jobs would become available again. It had been five years since their baby girl had died.

On December 31, Charlie Axel Stordahl was born. He weighed eight pounds and was strong and healthy. He was born with very blond hair; he certainly looked very Swedish.

Charlie was a good baby. They kept a warm hat on his head for they had to sleep in the upstairs bedroom where there was very little heat during the rest of the cold winter months.

America was really hurting all over the country. Those on rural farms did better than the city folk. People were hungry, looking for homes to live in, and employment. They began to wonder if the Depression would ever end.

A new president was voted on in November and began to open CCC camps. (CCC stands for Civilian Conservation Corps.) Dams were being built, new roads were constructed, and little by little, the Ford Motor Company began running again.

Charlie took his first steps on his first birthday. He was growing well due to his mother's milk to see him through his first year.

Charlie was baptized when the green grass grows, April 5, at the Covenant Church in Cheboygan by Rev. P. O. Lindman. Shortly after Charlie's first birthday, Eric's brother, Emanuel, called from Detroit, telling Eric that there were jobs now available at the Ford Motor Company. With Eric's experience at the garage, he should have no problem being hired. So the little family packed their few belongings and headed back to Detroit where they stayed at Emanuel's house and Eric obtained a good job at Ford's. After they got back on their feet financially, they moved back to their old home on Steel.

A new life was now ahead for them and they were so thankful that, at last, Eric had gone back to work. Charlie was running all over the house by now, exploring every nook and cranny that he could.

The country was slowly recovering from years of depression, joblessness, and hopeless situations. Eric was so glad that he had employment again. Charlie was the delight of their lives. He was adored by his parents, more so, because they had lost their first baby. Now they had something to live for, a little one that depended upon them to show him all the new things in life as they occurred.

It was wonderful to see a new life develop right before their eyes. Watching him take his first step, say his first word, smile at them, and make them laugh at his funny antics. At the age of three, Charlie was a talkative child, inquisitive, and curious to explore his own little world.

He loved playing in the sandbox that Eric had made for him, showing him how to make little roads for his little red car to ride on. The little boy next door, Tommy Brophy, came over to play once in a while. Eric made a swing on one of the branches of the peach tree and would take turns swinging the little boys up, up, and away. How they would laugh with delight and beg Eric to keep on swinging them.

When Charlie couldn't have his own way, he would stomp his right leg three times and turn around to go in his bedroom to play.

Eric spent much of the summer trying to teach the little boys to play catch and throw a softball. He had high hopes that some day the boys would play on a team especially for growing boys to develop their skills.

Holidays were always spent with the Stordahl aunts and uncles. He especially liked to go to Aunt Ruth's house in Pleasant Ridge. They made root beer from a special recipe.

Toward the end of the summer, several other boys would come over and join in the "Lets Play Catch Game." Colleen would always bring out lemonade and cookies for them to drink and eat.

In the fall, Charlie talked with his dad about getting a puppy for him to play with. Seems like most of his friends had a dog of their own that would fetch balls and do tricks of one kind or another. Eric told Charlie that it was late in the year and that when the green grass grows in the spring, it would be much better to get a puppy. The dog would have all spring and summer to become potty trained. This didn't set too good with Charlie, and he stomped his right foot three times and ran off to his bedroom to play with his toys.

Halloween came and went, and Thanksgiving at Uncle Elmer's came and went. Christmas at Aunt Esther's came and went. Charlie thought that "when the green grass grows" would never come.

Easter Sunday came in April of 1936. Charlie was now four years old. He got a new suit and little tie to wear to church after locating his Easter basket behind the couch. Easter was a fun time at church to watch all the ladies and girls with new Easter hats and bonnets. There was an Easter breakfast before church, and he ate his fill of ham and eggs, toast and jam.

After church, they went to Uncle Emanuel's house for Easter dinner. Eric told Charlie he had a surprise for him late Sunday afternoon, so Charlie patiently waited to see what that might be.

On the way home, they stopped at a house on Sorrento, and Eric came out holding a puppy in his arms. Charlie could hardly believe his eyes. He was so excited. His fat little cheeks held one great big happy grin. He was so happy.

The puppy was a Yorkshire terrier, eight weeks old. He was gold and black. He seemed to like his new owner immediately and wagged what was left of his little tail.

When they got home, Charlie quickly changed his clothes. Puppy and little boy went out to the backyard to spend what was left of the afternoon. Both boy and puppy lay down in Charlie's bed and took a nice long nap.

"What are you going to name your puppy, Charlie?" Eric inquired.

"Well, Daddy, I really liked Rudolph, the red-nosed reindeer, at Christmas. Can I call him Rudolph?" Charlie responded.

"Sure, son," Eric replied. So now the little puppy had a name, but they soon shortened the name to Rudy.

The rest of the summer, Charlie and Rudy romped and played in the backyard. They climbed the little hills in back of the house. Soon, the other boys brought their dogs over, and dogs and boys played fetch, chased balls, and played tag and other games until they were all tuckered out.

That fall, Eric and Charlie carved out pumpkins that they would use on Halloween for all the "Help the Poor" beggars who went from door to door to get candy and other treats to fill their shopping bags. Charlie dressed up like a hobo. There was a coal bin in the basement and Eric took some coal dust and smeared all over Charlie's face and hands. He also put some on his clothes to make him look like a hobo who hadn't taken a bath in a long, long time.

Charlie and his friend next door would go with an older sibling to go out "begging." Charlie got permission to take Rudy with him for the little dog would follow Charlie wherever he went. They went up one street and down another to see what they would receive from the different houses they went to. On the last street, Charlie and Tommy went up to the door and rang the bell. The owner laughed and laughed at the little boys and dropped some candy in their bags. As they went down the sidewalk, Charlie looked around for

Rudy, but he was nowhere to be found. Charlie and Tommy and Tommy's older sister called and called, but Rudy did not come. Charlie began to cry and stomp his right leg three times in frustration.

Tommy and Betty walked Charlie back home. He went in with his tear-stained cheeks, coal dust ran in streaks as tears soaked it. What a frightful-looking sight. Charlie explained the situation to his father, and the two of them went out to search for the puppy. He was almost full grown by now, but still was in his puppy days of learning. They searched for over an hour and went home down-hearted and sad for Rudy was still missing.

"Daddy, what can we do now to get Rudy back?" Charlie wanted to know.

"Well, son, I will put an ad in the paper, and you and I will go out when I get home from work each day and go look for him." Even these words from his dad made no difference. So that night, as they kneeled to pray, they both asked God to take care of him and bring him back home soon.

Things didn't go so well with Charlie. He missed his friend. He wondered if he would ever see him again. He continued playing with his little friends. Most of the time, it would be inside because it was getting cold outside. He hoped and prayed that Rudy was not cold, or sick, or hit by a car. He asked all his friends to keep watch for him

It would be another year before Charlie could go to school, which was five blocks away from where he lived. There was a candy store on Joy Road and Steel called Woods Ice Cream Shop. You could get a lot of candy there for a penny. He loved the wrapped Squirrel candies there. Eric took him there once a week to buy penny candy. Charlie loved the penny candy, but his dad always cautioned him not to eat too much.

Days went by. Charlie just didn't seem like the happy boy he used to be, and no matter what Colleen and Eric said, it didn't seem to make much difference.

The phone would ring and someone said they thought they saw the puppy here or there, but each time, it was not to be.

The peach tree in the backyard produced a large amount of fruit that fall, and Colleen canned peaches and made peach jam. Charlie loved to eat these big ripe peaches and have them on his cereal. He would watch his mother make jam and can peaches and make pies. He and Tommy would pick them off the ground and sit in the sandbox to devour their precious fruit. They took the pits and tried to place them on the roads and pretended they were houses or buildings where they could drive their little cars by.

"I miss my puppy," Charlie told Tommy. "Do you think I will ever get him back again?" Charlie really wanted to know what Tommy thought. Tommy, feeling sorry for his friend, tried to assure Charlie that Rudy would come back home. After all, by now, he would surely miss his little buddy that he loved so dearly. He told Charlie that he would be home before Charlie knew it. He just had to believe and it would happen. Charlie wanted to believe his friend and started to think that maybe if he believed really hard that Rudy would come back.

November came and Thanksgiving was soon approaching. Plans were made that they would go to Uncle Andrew's house this year. He lived on Monica Street.

So on Thanksgiving, they jumped into their Ford car, for that was the only kind of car Eric would buy since he worked for the Ford Motor Company, and they drove over to Monica Street.

They got there around one o'clock that afternoon. The adults sat around the living room and the children played in the basement. The smell of turkey permeated the air. The kids could hardly wait to taste the pumpkin pies piled high with whipped cream. Soon, they were all invited to sit down and eat.

Uncle Andrew prayed and the food was passed around. Everything looked so good. This was the first time in days that Charlie really ate a good meal. Playing with his cousins helped take his mind off the missing Rudy.

After eating the meal, each one around the table told of the things they were most grateful for. Some mentioned the end of the Depression, others for new jobs and homes. Some were thankful for new additions to the family. Seems like every year, there was a new cousin or two. Charlie didn't seem to say much about what he was grateful for.

The meal came to an end. He said good-bye to all his cousins, knowing he would see them again at Christmas time.

It was time to put on their coats and jackets and head for home. Charlie kept hoping that maybe they would see Rudy on the way home. He sat in the car waiting for his dad to come out, start it up, and take them back home.

On the way home from Thanksgiving dinner, Charlie was sitting in the backseat, musing. *What did I have to be thankful for—nothing! My puppy is still missing. Where is he? Will I ever see him again? I love him so much.* Then Charlie began to cry as if his heart would break.

"What's wrong, Charlie?" his mother asked. "Why are you crying?"

Through his sobbing and wailing, Charlie answered, almost unintelligibly, "I miss my Rudy…where is he? Will I ever see him again?"

Eric entered the conversation. "Charlie, God knows where Rudy is. He knows what happened to him. When we get home, we will walk through the neighborhood again. We will knock on doors. Someone knows about your doggy. Someone has seen him. I promise you that I will do everything I can to bring Rudy back."

"Okay, Daddy," Charlie answered. He trusted his father to keep his word. Charlie quieted down and soon dropped his head and fell asleep.

Colleen and Eric talked together, with great concern, on what they could do together to find little Rudy and bring him back again. The ten miles back home soon ended and they drove up their driveway, parking the car in the garage. Eric picked up Charlie and lay him on the couch until he woke up an hour later.

"Let's go, Charlie. We will take a walk around the neighborhood again and look for Rudy."

He put on his jacket and followed Eric out the front door. The weather was a bit nippy, but Charlie didn't care. He was going out to look for his missing friend. He took his father by the hand and the two began to canvass first on the street where they lived. Some folks were still celebrating Thanksgiving. They answered Eric's questions, but didn't offer much information. No one seemed to know or hadn't seen the little dog. They went on to the next street and the next, ringing bells, knocking on doors. It seemed to help Charlie to know that at least they were doing something about the situation. Two hours later with nothing but disappointing results, they returned home, rather exhausted, and Eric promised to do more telephone calling and getting others to be on the watch for Rudy.

Colleen tucked Charlie into bed that night and the two of them prayed that God would watch over Rudy until he was found. Soon, the little boy was fast asleep.

Friday dawned bright and sunny. There was about two feet of snow outside. The snow had accumulated over the course of a couple of weeks, but the roads were clear. There would still be a long winter ahead. Eric and Colleen sat at breakfast, still wondering how to cope with a seven-year-old boy whose dog was still missing. Soon, Charlie joined them and wondered if he and his dad would resume their search for Rudy.

Charlie returned to his bedroom and amused himself with his trucks and building blocks. Around 10:00 that morning, the phone rang. Colleen answered. It was Farmer Pete. He wanted to talk to Eric.

"Hello, Pete, what's new with you this morning?" Eric queried.

Farmer Pete told Eric that he had spotted a little dog behind the barn that morning. The dog ran off into the woods. His collie dog, Sandy, followed the dog. Pete had chores to do so he couldn't go out there to see if the dog was Rudy or not, but decided to give the Stordahls a call and see if Eric and Charlie would like to come over and walk through the woods to search for the missing dog. Eric told Pete that he and Charlie would be right over.

It didn't take long for Charlie to don his jacket and hat and run off to the Ford Model T parked in front of the house. His little heart started to beat hard in anticipation. His face glowed. "Dad, I hope and hope it is Rudy. It's got to be Rudy. Hurry, Dad, hurry!"

"I'm going as fast as I can, just be patient and we are soon there," Eric replied.

Charlie had grown quite a bit the last year. His little chubby legs had become long and slim. His hair had darkened to a light brown. He still had the same bright blue eyes and charming smile. He was a most delightful little boy to have around and to share his life with two loving parents.

Soon, they rounded the corner and drove into Farmer Pete's yard. Pete lived in a large white frame house where he had raised eight children. He had come to America in 1915. He had left Poland with his wife and two sons. Came to Detroit where manufacturing work had begun. He bought the farm with money he had saved in Poland. He knew when he died, the city would want his land for a subdivision to build homes. That farm of his would be the end of farming in Detroit.

Farmer Pete met them at the car, and they followed him to the small woods behind the large red barn where Pete milked ten cows morning and night. Chickens were running all over the yard. Charlie would love to spend some time on his farm and look around at all the animals and baby chicks and calves.

They tromped through the snow and saw paw prints that Sandy had probably made going into the woods.

"You better be real quiet, Charlie, remember Rudy has been missing almost a month and may be scared and run away from you. Let's all walk cautiously and be very quiet." They followed the paw prints, but they went in several directions. Seems Sandy loved to take walks in the wooded area. They avoided stepping on brush so it wouldn't make a crunching noise under their feet. They had gone about twenty-five yards when they spotted Sandy sleeping underneath an evergreen tree. Her front legs were sprawled out in front of her and lying between them was a little animal fast asleep.

Eric and Charlie walked very quietly and slowly, Eric holding on to Charlie's hand so he wouldn't go so fast. Sure enough, it was Rudy. Charlie leaned down and picked him up. The little dog was startled and began to yip, but Charlie held him close, petting him and crying. He was so happy. Sandy looked up at Rudy in Charlie's hands. It seemed like she could sense that this young lad knew the animal that Sandy had sheltered the past few weeks. What the story was, no one would ever know. One only could surmise that Sandy realized Rudy needed a friend, and for some reason, he showed up on the farm. How he made it so far away no one really knew.

Eric thanked Farmer Pete for letting him know all about the little dog he spotted in the back of his barn. Rudy was squirming for joy in Charlie's arms. It was a wonderful scene. A little boy reunited with his best friend after almost a month of being lost. Eric and Charlie got into the Ford and made their way back home. Colleen was elated when she saw Charlie coming up the drive to the house, clutching his friend tight in his arms.

The two of them played together, and finally Rudy, who was all worn out, lay down to take a much deserved nap. Charlie couldn't help but look at him over and over again. "I am so thankful, Mama, I never knew I could be so happy. I shall never let him out of my sight again."

"Charlie," Colleen uttered, "you have to allow him some leeway. He won't be a very happy dog if he can't have some freedom to run and play. Just be sure you know where he is when you come into the house. I think he has learned his lesson too, but don't be surprised if he runs over and sees his friend, Sandy, again. Maybe you could go there once a week. Farmer Pete said he would be glad to have you come over. You might even help him tend the farm."

"Okay, Mama, sounds like a good plan. I am always looking for something interesting to do."

1938

C harlie was seven years old now. It had been a long hard winter. One storm after the other hit the Detroit area. There were several days when school was canceled. One day was so bad, that Eric missed work. Charlie thought to himself that it would be a long, long time before the grass would turn green and he and his friends could play baseball at the new field near the school.

He tried to get over to Farmer Pete's farm at least once a week on Saturday. Rudy enjoyed these visits. He would frolic with Sandy and she would lick him and follow him all over. She truly had a mothering nature. Pete told Charlie that one time she brought home an abandoned baby bunny that he nurtured back to health. The rabbit was still there, having the run of the farm.

Charlie and his friends had built snowmen and forts, but that was getting old hat. He could only wait for the spring thaw and nature to restore the green grass. Along around the second week in April, the weather changed. Two whole weeks of high forties and low fifties temperature-wise melted the snow, and fields and lawns began to lose their snow. What a welcome sight!

Easter arrived and Charlie hunted all over the house for his Easter basket. Supposedly, the Easter bunny had visited, and now, the hiding place had to be discovered. At last, there it was in the oven in the kitchen. Rudy sat by his feet as he explored the contents of the basket. It seemed like a lot of chocolate bunnies and eggs, more than usual, were there waiting for Charlie to devour the tempting sweets.

They readied themselves for the Easter Service at church. When they arrived, the altar was decorated with blooming Easter lilies. Ladies and little girls donned new Easter hats and bonnets. Joy and happiness filled the air as those parishioners anticipated the symbols in the message to relate to the joy the disciples and women felt when they discovered the empty tomb and that Christ had risen from the dead.

Afterward, they motored to the elder Stordahl home for Easter dinner. Ham aroma filled the air. There were twenty-four present. Charlie took off his new Easter jacket and sat down to devour his Easter dinner. They returned home around four o'clock, and Rudy met them at the door, wagging his tail to welcome them back home. That afternoon, Eric and Charlie practiced ball in the backyard. It was rather chilly so after throwing, catching, and batting for an hour, they called it quits. Soon, the days would get longer, and Charlie and his buddies would gather together for work-outs in the Stordahl backyard.

In early May, the weather broke. Temperatures were in the high sixties. The grass was growing and had turned green. Now was the time to move ball practices to the school ball field. That's where Charlie and his gang would go on Saturday afternoons. Eric told them they had to find a name for the team. Eric's job would be to have other coaches get together teams for them to play. After practice, they gathered around Eric, sitting on the ground. They needed a name. One boy, Tommy Brophey, suggested the name "Winners." Eric said they would have to earn that name by winning games, but that wasn't the chief reason for the games. It was to develop character, sportsmanship, becoming good losers (if and when that occasion would happen), and to know it took lots of work and practice to develop good ball principles.

Ken Hanson suggested "Flying Eagles."

Dick Flemming suggested "Bull Dogs."

Vern Hart said, "How about McFarlane Giants?"

Other voices chimed in, but they couldn't agree, as a team, on any one of them.

There were eighteen boys present so Eric divided them into two teams to play each other in a practice session. All took turns pitching, batting at the plate, playing the bases, working the outfields, and catching the balls. After two hours, they were all exhausted and decided to go home. Eric was really satisfied with the work-out. Charlie could hardly wait until the first game in June. Eric took Charlie to Wood's Candy and Ice Cream shop for a cone before they went home. While they were there, Eric and Charlie discussed names for the team.

"You know, Dad, when we practice we race around the bases, we race around the outfield, we race to home plate to score runs, we spend a lot of time racing around. How about calling the team the McFarlane Racers?"

"You know, Charlie," Eric said, "That's really good thinking, we will bring that up at our next practice and see what the boys think about that name."

So the following Saturday, at practice, the subject was brought up and all the boys agreed on the name.

Then they all began racing around the field, yelling, "We are the Racers, we are the Racers."

In two weeks, it would be time for the first game. Eric told the boys they would be playing the Flying Tigers and Henry Jones would be their coach. The boys all left, anticipating that first game. School would be out the end of May. The green grass was really growing, getting ready to be mowed by Farmer Pete. Charlie was a very happy young lad. He just knew his team would win lots of games this summer.

The first game on the new ball field will always be remembered by Charlie. He got two hits and drove in a run. The Racers won the game by a score of seven to six. After the game, Eric took the boys to Wood's Candy and Ice Cream shop where each boy was treated to a cone. There would always be practice sessions during the week. Charlie was a very happy boy. He looked forward to a long summer where the green grass would grow and exciting things would happen.

He and Rudy visited Farmer Pete quite often. He and Rudy would walk through the little hills of Littlefield Street. They would see pheasants and rabbits as they walked along. He would pick up little stones to see how far he could throw them. Whenever they got close to the farm, Sandy would race out to greet them. Rudy and Sandy would race off together and always beat Charlie to the farm.

They would look around until they found Farmer Pete who would throw Charlie up in the air and let him rest on the back of his shoulders and would race around the yard, bouncing Charlie up and down. Charlie would laugh with each bounce. Then he would put Charlie down and they would go exploring any new event that would happen on the farm. He would place Charlie on the back of Princess, the pony, and let him ride until Charlie was exhausted. Farmer Pete was beginning to tan from being out in the sun. He loved Charlie and always looked forward to his visits.

One day in late June, as Charlie was exploring Farmer Pete's farm, he suddenly heard a loud yipping. Sandy charged out, racing to Charlie, barking for his attention. Charlie followed Sandy and found Rudy yipping away. It was evident the little dog was in pain and very, very scared. He approached the little dog and saw he was all tangled up in an electric fence wire that was lying on the ground. Someone had gone through the fence, bringing down the wire to the ground.

Charlie turned around and raced to find Farmer Pete. Sandy stayed by Rudy's side to try and comfort her little friend. Charlie found Pete out behind the barn and he started screaming at the top of his lungs. "Farmer Pete, hurry, Rudy is all tangled up in an electric wire lying on the ground. There is a big hole in the fence!"

Farmer Pete ran into the barn and turned the power off to the fence. Then the two of them ran to where the dog was. They found Rudy on the ground.

His little body was limp, but they could see he was still breathing. Farmer Pete untangled the wire from his body and lifted him up. He gave him over to Charlie, who hugged him close to his chest. Charlie began to sob. He thought for sure his little friend was gone and would no longer be with him. Sandy sat by his side, whining, as if she was in sorrow too.

Farmer Pete put his arm around Charlie's shoulders and led him back to the farm.

"Someone or something busted through that fence. I will have to repair it before the cows get home. I will take you and

Rudy home. Let me know how things go with your doggie. I think he will be all right. He probably passed out from the pain. He is still breathing. Just keep holding him close. It wouldn't hurt to say a little prayer for him."

Charlie did just that, but it wasn't a little prayer. It was a long, somber prayer. He took Rudy into the house and showed the dog to his mother. She was quite upset when she heard of Rudy's ordeal. She took Rudy and began massaging his chest. In a few minutes, Rudy opened his eyes and began to wag his tail. Charlie was so happy, he began crying for joy. He still had his little dog with him. He told Colleen about the electric fence and the mishap that took place.

She called Farmer Pete and thanked him for taking care of her son and his dog. She told him to let her know if he found out who or what had crashed through his fence.

Charlie and his cronies did many things together that summer. When it was hot and dry, they took turns at each others homes, running through the sprinklers to cool off. They played kick-the-can in the street and hand ball at their homes, throwing the ball against the walls in various forms. They started out by throwing once and catching the ball, then letting the ball bounce once, twice, and three times off the wall before catching it. Lifting one leg and letting the ball bounce off the wall. For twelve times, various methods of throwing and catching the ball would take place. The one that finished first would be the winner.

Once, they all brought an orange and tossed it gently against the wall until it became really juicy inside, and then they would suck the juice out. They loved climbing trees, playing hide-and-seek, and a game called run-my-sheepy-run. Mothers would take popsicle sticks and put them into Kool-Aid ice cubes and give all the kids a treat. Boys and girls together would play these games and indulge in these treats. Kids in the neighborhood bonded themselves in meaningful relationships. Some boys would put up tents in the backyard and invite other boys to sleep over and roast hot dogs around the camp fire.

These children did not know what it was like to milk a cow, use an outhouse, not have electric lights and wood ranges, or gather chicken eggs like kids brought up on a farm, but Charlie, visiting Farmer Pete, got acquainted with these outdoor chores. He even had a wood range that he cooked on.

One day, Rudy went over to visit Farmer Pete and he took Charlie and Rudy to a hill in back of his dairy farm. As they sat there, Farmer Pete began to tell Charlie what it had been like to be raised in Poland, which was now called Prussia.

"When I came here, Charlie, I had to stay in the lower part of the boat that brought us over here from Poland. It took eight weeks to get here. Each one of us brought some food with us that we shared with each other. This was the only thing we had to eat until we landed in New York at Ellis Island. Can you imagine what that was like, Charlie?"

"No, I have never had to go without food for any length of time," Charlie replied.

Farmer Pete looked at Charlie with a slight frown on his face. Rudy sat between the two of them as if he were taking in all that was said and enjoying being with his two buddies.

Farmer Pete continued, "It was really awful, but we had our minds set on going to America where there was freedom and people could own property that belonged to them instead of working for a noble man. Sometimes, in order to conserve food, which was mostly beans and oatmeal, we would only eat once a day. Some would get sea sick and others come down with colds and fever. We buried several people at sea. They just weren't strong enough to make the long journey. When we saw the Statue of Liberty, our hearts beat with expectation, and at last, the long stressful boat ride was over with."

Charlie breathed a sigh of relief. "I am so glad you came here, I am so glad you have this farm here. I just love coming here. Can you tell me more stories about where you came from? I just love listening to your stories," Charlie stated emphatically.

When Charlie got home, he told his mom and dad all that Farmer Pete went through to get here in Detroit. He said he would tell me more true stories about Poland.

"That's great, Charlie, but your mother and I had similar experiences that our relatives went through to get here. America is a great haven for poor destitute emigrants from all over Scandinavia, Ireland, and Europe," Eric told him.

SHIRLEY BERGSTROM

Colleen put her arm around Charlie and said, "Son, my relatives came from Ireland. There are many hardships they endured too. Once a week, before you go to bed, I will tell you what it was like for them to live in Ireland. These stories should make you realize what a wonderful land you are living in. All the stripes in our flag have a story to tell. We had to fight for our independence from England. That's why your classes in history should be so interesting."

Charlie was interested. He looked forward to all these storytellers tell him of his heritage. These stories would shape his life and make him the man that his parents could be proud of.

That night, Eric put Charlie to bed and started his story about Sweden. "My grandparents came to America from Sweden in 1882. Grandpa's sister and Grandma's brother-in-law lived next door to each other. Yes, Charlie, sister and brother married the other's sister and brother. They were double cousins. In Sweden, they grew up in crofts. This was land owned by rich landowners who would build houses for their workers who would farm the land. Much of the crops they raised would be taken over by these landowners."

Charlie nodded off to sleep, and in his dreams, he was in another land. Eric watched as his son slept and reminisced about his own life. How lucky he felt to have a little boy.

Another winter passed as well as another spring. Now it was May 9, and Eric and Colleen became parents again. Judith Elizabeth Stordahl entered the world to the delight of her father and mother. Charlie looked into the little face of his baby sister and wondered why this squirming, bawling baby was so alluring to his mom and dad.

Charlie still had his dog, Rudy, to talk to. They would always remain good buddies. Rudy was his faithful friend. He spent much of his time that summer (1939) playing with his friends and enjoying ball games at the school ball field where his dad still coached the ball team. Of course, he and Rudy would still go over and visit Farmer Pete.

"Hey, Charlie, come with me to the barn, I have something to show you," Pete exclaimed.

The two and Rudy hurried to the barn so Charlie could see some newborn pups that Sandy had given birth to a few days ago.

"Here they are, Sandy's new pups born on May 9. Look at this one, isn't she sweet?"

Charlie picked up the tiny pup and started to pet her. "That's when my sister was born," Charlie said.

"She's far cuter than my new baby sister and more fun to hold, but I suppose, when she gets bigger, I will be a good brother for her. Who knows, we may even be good friends some day."

He put the puppy down next to Sandy, and Pete and Charlie went off to their favorite place to talk. There at the top of the hill, the two sat down for their oft time talks.

"Tell me, Farmer Pete, what was it like living in Poland?"

"Where my father and mother were born near Warsaw, times were pretty bad," Pete related. "There was a potato famine all over Europe and Scandinavia. People stayed pretty close to home. Sometimes, the neighbors would gather together to make homemade cheese or help each other with corn and wheat crops. In the year 1878, the weather was extremely dry. There was very little rain. Only a few potatoes were harvested and they were small. Not much of anything was harvested that year and the noblemen made it pretty clear that there was very little they could add to the family's meals. Times were very trying. Once, my grandmother made soup out of potato skins and took a sole off a worn-out boot and put it in the pot with the skins for added flavor. That's what the family had for supper that night."

"Oh goodness," Charlie uttered. "I could never eat that kind of soup."

Pete replied, "There was a lot of nourishment in the skins and it did fill the tummies so they could sleep that night. At night, they slept on mattresses made of straw and pillows filled with duck down. Most everything they had was made by hand. Even the house they lived in was made with sod and clay for there was very little timber around to build houses. Outbuildings were also made of sod, and the roofs were made of straw and called thatched roofs. When you entered the house, you stepped down about eight inches to the floor of the foundation. Houses were small and most of the family slept in one or two bedrooms. Sometimes, straw mattresses were placed right on the floor of the house."

All of this was very hard for Charlie to imagine, but he sure was thankful for his own bed.

4

As the afternoon wore on, Farmer Pete noticed dark clouds in the west approaching fast.

"Better head for home, Charlie, its getting dark and the wind is picking up. It's going to rain soon."

Charlie and Rudy got up and started for home with a fast walking pace for a little boy. It wasn't long before thunder rolled across the sky and lightning bolts began to strike here and there.

"Hurry, Rudy, let's go fast." Off they went at a faster clip. Then the rain pelted down, and in no time at all, the two of them were drenched. Charlie ran even faster, and then he noticed Rudy wasn't running beside him any longer. He turned around and called his name, but there was no response.

He backtracked for a few yards when he noticed a huge bird ascend from the ground. Charlie ran to the spot and there was his little friend, wet, bedraggled, and bleeding from a torn cheek. He knelt beside the wounded dog and began crying. "Whatever happened, Rudy?" His jaw was ripped almost to his cheek, and he lay there whimpering. Charlie picked him up, mopping wet rain off his brow. His hair was dripping water all over him. It was hard running now and carrying a wounded animal besides. He was really tired when he went through the back door of his home. He called for his mom and she came from the living room with baby Judy in her arms. She took one look at the dog and told Charlie that he needed stitches and medical attention. At 4:30 p.m., Eric came home from work. He was told about Rudy's injury.

And Eric picked the dog up and carried him to the car with Charlie following behind.

It took about twenty minutes to get to the veterinarian's office. They waited in the waiting room until the vet could take a look at him. About half an hour later, they were ushered into a room where they could lay Rudy on the table.

Dr. Dobias looked him over and said, "Yes, he will need stitches, but look here at your dog's back. There are four talon punctures where some large bird tried to carry him away." Charlie and Eric looked through the fur where the doctor showed them the puncture marks. Each one would require stitches and a cleaning of the wounds to prevent infection.

"Wow, no wonder he was whimpering, he's hurt really bad."

The doctor told them to leave the room while he attended to the wounds that needed stitches.

They waited patiently for Rudy to get the stitches. At least, the doctor agreed that a large bird, either an eagle, owl, or chicken hawk had done the grizzly damage to their little friend. After what seemed like ages, the nurse came out and told them Rudy was ready to go home. They entered the room and picked up Rudy, paid the bill, and headed back home.

Rudy lay in his little bed for the rest of the day, sleeping off the anesthetic.

Around 7:00, Farmer Pete invited them over Saturday night to enjoy a Polish feast with all of his Polish relatives. He told Colleen that Charlie took a real interest in learning all about Polish traditions and life there in Poland. Colleen told him they would come if she could bring some Swedish and Irish dishes. Pete thought it would be a wonderful idea to share their ethnic traditions together.

They could all learn a lot about other nationalities and it would really be good for Charlie. After all, they were really all Americans and it would be wonderful to share with each other all the good things about the countries they came from. Charlie was really pleased and Colleen sat down and wrote down all the things she would fix and would make a list of items needed from the grocery stores. Their favorite place to shop was Krogers. Then she would have to go to a Swedish store to buy lingon berries and lute fisk. The Stordahls were really excited about the weekend together with other nationalities at Farmer Pete's.

5

Colleen put on an Irish bonnet and dress. She dressed Charlie up in knickers and a blue and yellow shirt. Eric wore a hat his father had worn in Sweden. They piled into the black Ford family car and headed for the Socolovitchs.

When they arrived, there were cars parked all over. Long boards were placed on sawhorses for the people to sit on. There was a large table where the food had been placed and Colleen was shown where to place her ethnic dishes. Farmer Pete said the blessing and the women stood besides the dishes of food they brought to explain what the ingredients were and what they were called. Charlie was thrilled beyond measure even though he had to leave his friend home to mend from his ordeal.

Phyllis Stempky told the Stordahls she brought perogies and sweet sour cabbage; Colleen told the Polish people she had brought Swedish sausage (korve) and Irish soda bread, kraup kraukas (potato dumplings stuffed with ham), a Swedish tea ring and lute fisk, also lingon berries to put on angel food cake. Ruby Romanik brought fruit-filled pastries and stuffed cabbage. Eric brought over from the car a large pot of Irish stew. What a feast and how they loaded their plates with all the tempting ethnic dishes. After dinner, Colleen did an Irish jig with Eric. Eric showed them some Swedish folk dances and all the Polish people got up to polka. The fiddles played and people laughed and joked, ate some more, danced some more, and really had a great time. Farmer Pete was pleased with the way things were going. Then the people told each other about things that they did in their homelands. They all agreed that the towns they came from were very small, maybe a grocery store and a post office. They like to go shopping on Saturday nights and talk at the general store. Life in all their countries settled around the small churches where the bell would ring every Sunday morning to call them to worship. All the churches had small pump organs and a hymnal with hymns of that country sung during the services. After the service, men would gather on one side of the church and the women and children on the other side to share the week's events that happened at their homesteads. Then they would all pile into the wagons pulled by their family horses and head for their homes for family dinners together. It was amazing how much alike the Sundays were in each of their countries. Charlie got to play with lots of boys his age. They played hide-and-seek, tag, and run-my-sheepy-run. Charlie would never forget this night as long as he lived.

He also learned that almost half the people of Poland immigrated to America in the late 1880s and over one-third of all Swedes left their homeland. Colleen said there were many of Irish descent that left Ireland, but she didn't know how many. It was late that evening before people left to go back to their homes, but Pete was so pleased and there really seemed to be a lot of smiles on people's faces as they got into their cars instead of horses and buggies that seemed to be fading from history.

The rest of the summer was spent at the Sunday school picnic where there were three-legged races, sack races, regular running races, and other contests that kids love. Someone had made a large man made out of wood that stood up so that the ladies could throw rolling pins at him. Each one that knocked him down won a prize. Then there was a throwing of shoes contest. The one that threw their shoe the farthest was given a prize. The men loved the pie-eating contest, and Uncle Andrew Stordahl won that contest. The picnic ended with a ball game made up of teenage boys and young men.

After that, there was the eating of watermelon. Charlie tried to gobble his down first, but Cousin Harold finished first.

Then, there was the ball game tournaments, with his team winning the championship, and they were all treated to ice cream sundaes at Woods Store on West Chicago and Steel.

Baby Judy was growing fast and Charlie really liked being her big brother. She would laugh and giggle every time he paid attention to her. Rudy was fully recovered from his ordeal with the big bird and happily followed Charlie wherever he went.

Farmer Pete called one day and told Eric it was teenage hooligans that kicked his fence down. Seems like they were getting into trouble all over the neighborhood. Charlie couldn't understand how they could be so mean when there was so many other fun things to do.

6

Before Charlie had reached his tenth birthday, the school children at McFarlane Elementary School were called to a special meeting in the auditorium. The school principal got up and spoke, "Boys and girls, a very tragic event has occurred to our nation. Yesterday morning, December 7, 1941, Pearl Harbor in Hawaii was bombed by Japanese aircrafts that flew over the waters, destroying most of the American warships anchored there. The attack was certainly not expected and really caught our Navy off guard and it took awhile for our seamen to retaliate. Several of the Japanese aircraft were shot down, but not until 3,000 lives were lost and most of the ships. Panic and fear gripped the people of the island. The scene afterward was complete chaos. Sailors were drowned on the sinking ships. Pearl Harbor was a dreadful scene. Our president, Franklin Roosevelt, declared war against Japan. Boys and girls, a lot of you don't know what it is like for a country to go to war, but you will find out in days to come that the American people will pull together and make sure this enemy is defeated. Don't worry, students, let the adults do the worrying. You just continue to study and be good students. We will win this war, with God's help and American determination. We will defeat the enemy and make our land a safe place for all you children to grow up in."

After the principal's talk, the students were dismissed to go home for he knew they would be upset and needed Mama and Papa's help to get them through this terrible time for America.

Eric read in the papers day after day and week after week the progress of the war. Soon, it was decided that America should declare war against Germany. Young men enlisted in the Army, Navy, and Marines all over the United States. Many young men in their senior year in high school left to go into the service of their country to defeat the enemy. Eric and Colleen constantly reassured Charlie that everything was going to be all right. Little Judy was too young to realize all that was going on, but Charlie knew and this would be the time of his young life that he would never forget.

Soon, the government was selling war bonds and people from all walks of life were buying them. Stockings with seams down the back were of short supply and women had to go without to support the war effort. Women were asked to render their lard and give it to the government for the sake of the war. In churches in the vestibule, the names of all men who enlisted in the service were placed on the walls so the congregation could pray for them. It was a time that united Americans to pull together to win the war.

Women were hired in the manufacturing industries to take the places of the men who had enlisted to serve their country.

Charlie remembered often the times the air raid sirens would go off and everyone had to turn out all their lights. If they didn't, the air raid warden would knock on their door and give them a citation. Sometimes, these drills would last quite awhile. No one knew whether or not if German aircraft or the Japanese aircraft would fly over and bomb them. This was a very trying time. President Roosevelt would speak on the radio many times to let the people know how brave they were and how thankful he was that they were supporting the war effort. Charlie would listen to the president's speeches, feeling awestruck.

Then gas was rationed, sugar was rationed. There were reports daily in all the papers on how the war was progressing, how many died in the service to their country. Charlie remembered going to church, and it seemed, almost every week, there would be another name added to the list of those that gave their lives for their country. It wasn't only America that was at war, it seemed like the whole country was at war. Charlie starting hearing the phrase "World War II" mentioned among the adults. No one could ignore this war. Some thought that this would be the war to end all wars. Adults discussed the daily events and Charlie would listen in. He didn't want to miss anything. Rudy remained his faithful friend even when Charlie sat on the stairs to hear what his parents were saying.

Farmer Pete came over one day and told Eric and Colleen that Poland had succumbed to the Germans. He said there were concentration camps there now where Jews were being sent to be gassed in the gas chambers. The Jews hadn't lived in Israel since the Romans took over in the year AD 70 when they had to leave and go to the nations of the world to survive. It seemed that Hitler hated the Jews, and wherever they conquered a nation, Jews in that country were executed. Pete felt bad for the people of Poland. Before World War I, the Polish people were under the rule of Russia and were liberated at the end of that war. Now they were conquered by another fiend named Hitler who was a mad man bound to exterminate the Jewish population. Pete had tears in his eyes when he left. He felt so bad for his people. Whatever would happen to them?

So now was the time for the people of America to unite in prayer for the defeat of this tyrant that seemed to be taking over many, many countries week after week. This was the topic of prayer at Wednesday night prayer meetings.

Papers were filled with pictures of war scenes. There was the bombing of London, the bombing of Paris, just to name a couple of places. Hitler's armies were on the move. All over America, war songs were written: "When the Lights Go On All Over the World," "The Boys Come Home Again All Over the World," "We're Coming in on a Wing and a Prayer," "There'll Be Blue Birds over the White Cliffs of Dover Tomorrow When the World Is Free," "Anchors Aweigh," and many, many more.

7

In the spring of 1942, when the green grass grows, Eric and Colleen bought a new house between the Arteries of Schaefer on the East and Greenfield on the South and Joy Road on the North and Tireman on the South. They had been saving their money for a long time to make the down payment of $500. The home was priced at $5,500. This was a great new adventure in their lives.

They sat down with Charlie and explained the whole move and why they had to do it, hoping the little fellow would understand that this was a necessary step in planning their future in Detroit during this war. Henry Ford was donating parcels of land to their employees to plant Victory Gardens to aid in the production of vegetables during shortages which could occur to help feed the armies which were deployed all over Europe and Asia to free nations from the tyranny of Japan and Germany. Not only that, but it was better to own their own home than to rent and not show anything for it.

"You mean I have to leave all my friends, my ball team, Farmer Pete, and the school I am growing up in?" Charlie spoke in a choked-up voice.

"Yes, Charlie, but you will meet new friends," Eric replied, "and you will go to a new school, and who knows, what good things will happen to you when we move?"

Charlie got up and stomped his right leg three times and went off to his bedroom with his dear friend Rudy. He went over to Farmer Pete's the next day and told him the news. Pete was sorry his good little chum would be leaving, but he assured Charlie that everything would work out all right. Charlie was not so sure about that, but he hugged his dear friend and tears started to run down his cheeks. Pete held him close and told him that he could come and visit anytime that he wanted to.

The Stordahls began packing articles into boxes and rented a moving van to haul all their belongings to Robson Street. Men from the church came and helped with the move. That night, they spent their first night in their new home. Charlie got a big room in the attic and little Judy had her bedroom on the same floor as Eric and Colleen. Charlie tossed and turned all night, shedding a few tears and holding Rudy close to his side.

The next day, he and Rudy ventured out to explore the new neighborhood. He saw a school south of his home in the next block. By one side road was a new school and on the south side road was a portable two-room school. He wondered which one he would go to. The portable school was rather uninviting and he sure didn't want to go there. He looked for boys his age to play with. Going by one house on the way home was a boy who looked to be his age. He stopped and talked to him and found out his name was Bobby Lockheart. He had an older sister named Maureen. She had red hair and freckles and dark hair and eyes. He talked to them for several minutes, and Bobby told Charlie that in the summer, they would be playing ball in the street and invited him to join them.

Charlie walked down the next block and met another boy named Richard Callio. This boy was one he could walk to school with when it started in the fall. He told Charlie he would come by later and go bike riding with him and show him other things in the neighborhood. He was a happy young lad with blond hair and blue eyes and seemed like a fun-loving boy.

When Charlie got home, he told his mom about the two boys he met, and Colleen told him his dad was going to put a sandbox in the backyard for little Judy and he could help his sister adjust to staying in a fenced-in backyard. Then the lady next door came over and told them her name was Grace

Garbacz and her husband's name was Stan. She talked with a Polish accent, which reminded him of Farmer Pete. Stan had come over from Poland, taken a course in English, and settled in Detroit because that's where the jobs were. They had only been living here since 1940 and were quite distraught when the war broke out. They had a daughter, Laurette, who was a teenager. Grace had light-brown hair and hazel eyes. She wore an apron and seemed to be a nice person.

Charlie told his mother that it would be hard for him to live here because he still would miss his friends, but he would try the best he could to make new friends and get used to a new house where there was no one living down below them that he would have to share the house with.

In June, the church moved from Fourteenth and Antoinette to Dexter and Davison, so now, Charlie would have to adjust to a new church. No longer would they be riding by the gas station with the flying red horse. The new church was closer to where they lived. Gas rationing was in full swing so they would be able to use less when going to the new church.

Two weeks later, Eric took Charlie out to his Victory Garden way out Michigan Avenue not far from Greenfield Village. It was a big enough plot to plant a few tomatoes, peppers, and onion sets. Eric planted beets, peas, green beans, and one row of corn. He would take Charlie with him during the summer to help weed and water the garden. Charlie liked this time together with his dad. Judy was only two and not big enough to help with the garden.

In the entryway of the church, a new board was put up with those that died in the service of various branches of armed forces. Two of his cousins, Lloyd and Allen, were now added to the list, and every Sunday, prayers were said for the Lord to intervene and bring victory to the Allied Forces and the boys to come home.

Women were now being hired to take the place of the men in the factories who had enlisted in the armed forces. Other women, nurses, were being inducted to help with the wounded in various parts of the world. More war songs were being written and sung. Bob Hope and his entourage were going overseas to put on shows for those serving the United States of America. Kate Smith was singing "God Bless America" and other patriotic songs over the radio. It was a time when America was united and all pledged to do their best for the war effort.

In churches all over America, hymns for the freedom of the nation were sung. One of the favorites was "The Battle Hymn of the Republic" and also, "America the Beautiful."

People sang with gusto.

Charlie didn't like when air raid sirens sounded their alert and lights went out all over Detroit. Sometimes, it was for short periods, and other times for long periods. He would go outside and stand on the sidewalk and the only light that could be seen was from the moon and stars. Detroit was in a blackout. Sometimes, it made Charlie shudder.

He started school that fall in the Parkman Portable School. You entered into a big room with a large wood and coal furnace in the middle. On the wall were hooks to hang your jackets on. He sat next to Richard Callio. On the corner of his desk was an inkwell to hold the fluid for his ink pen. This all seemed strange to Charlie. MacFarlane wasn't anything like this dump. In the wintertime, the ink would freeze in the inkwell, and it was several hours before he could dip his pen in and write.

In the year 1944, on May 21, the war came to an end, but prior to that, the army and navy freed island after island in the Pacific from Japan. The islands of Corregidor, the Philippines, Wake, Iwo Jima, and others. Then unbeknownst to the public, the United States bombers dropped the atomic bomb on Nagasaki and Hiroshima and thousands of Japanese lost their lives and made havoc of the countryside. It was a horrible disaster area. The Japanese were scared to death and Japan gave up.

Several months later was D-Day. This would be the now or never part of the final battle with Germany. On the shores of Omaha Beach in France, the Allied Forces landed. Airplanes filled the sky and dropped down the paratroopers, barge after barge of Marines, and soldiers raced over the beaches for the German forces were bombarding them with artillery strikes. Many lost their lives and lay dead on the beaches of

Normandy. They kept coming and coming, and soon, the German army had to retreat. Two thousand French soldiers, along with the United States armies, lost their lives.

As the Army advanced, they went from house to house to liberate the people there and then from town to town until all of France was free. The United States armies freed the people of Poland, England, and other war-torn territories.

A large cemetery was put aside by France for the bodies of the fallen soldiers who had given their lives for freedom. Each grave had a white cross with a flag from the country in which they had lived. This cemetery was called Flanders Field where French and American soldiers were laid to rest.

Needless to say, Americans rejoiced every day when the world was liberated from the unmerciful Hitler and all his cohorts who had caused so much bloodshed and devastation to the countries of the world. Farmer Pete and all his relatives were so thankful that Poland was now free to be Poland. There were parades in every town and cities across America. People were running up and down the streets shouting out, "We are free! We are free!"

The pastors who had served as chaplains were now looking for churches to pastor. All the war-torn nations of the world were celebrating and America would help them to rebuild that which had been lost.

Charlie was thirteen when the World War II ended and would enter McKenzie High School in the fall. He and Richard Callio would ride the bus together. His homeroom number was 316. There were three floors to the high school, a swimming pool, and an industrial arts lab for the boys. One could take driver's training right on school property. It was an exciting time for Charlie. He was now in his teens, a young man, and childhood behind him. Before school started, his little sister, Judy, was now five years old. One morning, she woke up with a high fever and was very listless. Colleen and Eric were very concerned. During summers in Detroit, a dreaded disease called polio was striking family after family, causing legs and arms to grow numb and not be able to function anymore. Many were dying, especially children, from this sickness.

They took Judy to Dr. Ross B. Richardson for a diagnosis. He told Eric and Colleen, "I am afraid your daughter has come down with polio."

This dropped like a bombshell to their ears.

"Oh no!" Colleen screamed.

She clutched Judy in her arms, talked over with the doctor as what they should do about this, and left with grief flooding through their minds and hearts. They sat in silence as they motored back to their home.

Once they were back home, they took Judy into the living room and took turns rocking her in the rocking chair Eric had made. Charlie could feel the sadness in the home and he prayed really hard that Judy would be okay. He even held her and rocked her.

The next day, Judy could hardly move. Her paralysis made it difficult to get her to drink. Her listless eyes caused deep pain for her parents.

Two days later, little Judy was gone. Colleen broke down and cried. Deep anguishing cries that rocked the entire house. Charlie went to his room and cried. He held on to his good friend Rudy and sobbed and sobbed until he fell asleep.

Funeral arrangements were made with the funeral home and Rev. Albert Bengtson. The church filled with members, friends, and relatives of the grieving family. Charlie tried to be brave and not cry, but he succumbed to his sadness and sobbed. His adorable baby sister was gone. The pastor said she was in heaven. That she was no longer in pain or suffering. That she was safe in the arms of Jesus, but he would still miss this little being who had looked up to him so much. He had read bedtime stories to her and wiped away her tears when she fell and hurt herself. It just wouldn't be the same without her. Even Farmer Pete was there to offer his sympathy.

They went home sad and grieving. It would take several days before they began to recover. They just had to remember that now, heaven was a real place to them for Judy was there waiting for them to come and join them someday. Grief stricken, the family knew life had to go on.

Charlie was a good student in school. He wanted to be an engineer. Jobs all over Detroit were asking for men to apply for these positions. He met a young lass in high school whose name was Josephine O'Sullivan. He met her in the English class where he learned to write stories and essays. He would walk her to her next class and they would have lunch together. Charlie wasn't allowed to date until he was sixteen, so they settled for being in class together and eating in the cafeteria each day. Before school started each day, they would meet by the flag pole and talk until school started.

Josie lived on Sorrento in his old neighborhood but didn't remember ever seeing her or seeing her at school. He had been so involved with ball games and boys at school that he didn't have an eye for the girls.

He had a lot of homework every day and spent evenings doing his homework. He studied hard and long, so he would become good college material.

He would go with his dad and mother to the Ford Rotunda at Christmas time. There was always a Christmas performance to see, many Christmas decorations, and snacks. A lot of friends from the neighborhood were there. It was good to sing the Christmas carols and talk and snack and just have a fun time during the evening. Greenfield Village was always lit up for Christmas and the museum was open with all its antiques and displays.

They put up the tree a week before Christmas, but there was no little Judy to help with the trimming and no little girl presents under the tree. Sadness would come on the family from time to time, especially holidays, and opening presents just wouldn't be the same this year.

When Charlie was fifteen and a junior in high school, tragedy struck the Stordahl family again. On May 15, when the green grass grows, Eric read the headlines of the *Detroit Free Press*: "Last Farmer of Detroit Was Homicide Victim." In the column below was an article.

> Farmer Pete Socolovitch was found out near his barn, a victim of foul play. He had been strangled with a rope lying near his body. He is the last farmer to own property here in Detroit. He sold milk to the Sealtest Dairy. He will be greatly missed as a neighborhood friend to those living on the West Side of Detroit. Police are scouting the neighborhood for the murderer.

A picture of Farmer Pete was underneath the article. Charlie read it and stomped his right leg three times, took Rudy out in the backyard, and wept until he could cry no more.

The funeral was held at the end of the week at the funeral home. His body was laid to rest at the Evergreen Cemetery not very far from Judy's grave. On Decoration Day, May 30, he and Eric, Colleen, and the Socolovitches all came and planted flowers on their loved ones' graves. Now Charlie didn't care if he ever went back to the old neighborhood. It would never be the same. 1947 would always be a bad year to remember.

He still liked to play ball with his friends. Several girls would also join in the fun. Summer was spent going to the

River Rouge Park Swimming Pool. Josie would meet him there. She rode by bus down Joy Road, and sometimes on Saturdays, Eric would let Charlie have the car and he would take her home. Most of the time, he would stay for supper, and afterward, they would sit on the front porch swing and talk until dark.

They would talk about their plans for the future. Josie wanted to be a nurse and would go to a school in downtown Detroit and intern at the hospital there.

The name Ford appeared on a lot of buildings: Ford Memorial Hospital, Ford Motor Company, Henry Ford Trade School, Ford Rotunda, etc.

Josie's parents were from Ireland, and one day, Colleen said to Charlie, "Pete told you all about Poland, now that you are older, I want to tell you all about Ireland. We will do this on Sunday afternoon, and Josie can come with you." So the agreement was made and now Charlie would be told about Ireland when the green grass grows.

On Friday of that week, another article appeared in the newspaper. It read:

> Police solve the mysterious death of the last farmer to live in Detroit. Three seventeen-year-old teenage boys have been arrested in the gruesome death of Farmer Pete. Clues left at the murder scene led to their arrest. George Wainwright, Kevin Freemont, and Alexander

Corriondow confessed after being interrogated by the police. They were sorry they had to kill the farmer's dog, Sandy, but she was attacking them to defend Pete. They admitted that they were responsible for heckling the farmer for the past three years. They had cut his fences, let out his cattle, opened the chicken coop, and threw tomatoes at his house. They didn't seem sorry for what they did—only that they got caught and were arrested. They would be held for trial some time in the fall.

"Well," said Charlie, "that's who was responsible for the cut fence I found one day when I was visiting Pete! I wonder why they did that. What was their reason for tormenting one of the best friends I ever had?"

Eric replied, "There's more down here in another paragraph. It said that they were tired of the smells coming from the farm. Their parents complained constantly that the odor was awful. Well, they won't have to complain any more, but now, their boys were facing prison sentences. I think they would be glad now to put up with the smells and have their sons back home. Life is strange here in Detroit. Seems like someone always has something to complain about."

After church on Sunday, Josie came over around three to listen to Colleen talk about Ireland where some of her relatives still lived. Josie had beautiful red hair and blue eyes. She was slim and around five foot three inches tall. Charlie's hair was getting darker like his dad's. He was almost six feet tall and of slender build. He was muscular from all of his sports activities. He had a charming smile and disposition, a real joy to his parents. Both of them wanted to hear all about Ireland and sat down around the dining room table to listen.

Colleen got out her book on Ireland and the first thing she said was, "When the green grass grows in Ireland, it becomes a lush green like you have never seen before. They love to groom their lawns and the neighborhoods become a wonder to behold. There are a lot of castles in Ireland. In Donegal, there is one made of stone." She pointed to the picture. "It had two side dormer windows atop with a center window. There was a fence all around and a side building abutting each other. There was a large lower window, side walks, and was the grave site of the poet, W. B. Yeats that had a beautiful old cross with intricate designs covering the entire middle of the cross. There is a castle in Bunratty. It was the last of four fortresses and overlooks the Shannon, which you will want to see. It is sung in Irish folk song, 'Where the River Shannon Flows.' It was built in the middle of the fifteenth century by a military chief Siod Mac Commara O'Briens. Kings and earls of Thomond ruled there for years. In 1646, the castle was captured by Admiral Penn. William Penn, founder of Pennsylvania, was just a tiny baby when he was brought here and lived for a time before going to America. They serve wonderful banquets here for visitors from all over to enjoy. Most castles endured because of their finely sculpted stones. It is a remarkable experience to visit the castles of Ireland.

And yes, there are lighthouses in Ireland too. They are white, black, and red. Ronald Reagan stayed at a castle. It's name was Cliden Co. Galway."

Colleen pointed to a picture of Saint Patrick. "He arrived in AD 432 as a slave. Ireland was proclaimed a republic in April 18, AD 49. He was noted for chasing the rats out of Ireland. Legend says that he prayed them out, but anyway, he is our patron saint, a real man of God. The flag of Ireland is white, a symbol of peace; orange for the Catholics; and green to represent the Protestant tradition. I think you have heard enough about Ireland for now. I have to go through my drawers and find out the rest of the information that I think you will be interested concerning Ireland."

They spent the rest of the afternoon outside on the porch talking about the heritage Charlie had and encouraged him to learn all he could about Sweden and Ireland. This would give him a longing to go and visit these lands of his parent's upbringing.

8

The next few years, Charlie and Josie continued their high school education.

They spent weekends roller skating at the River Rough Roller Dome, ice skating at the rink in back of Parkman School, going to Cedar Point (a place where there were amusement rides of all kinds). They also went to the Masonic Temple for Voice of Christian Youth Meetings, saw Roy Acuff and his Smokey Mountain boys at the Olympia Stadium, went to the Tiger ball games. There were Young People Meetings at the Covenant Church. These were held every Sunday night in the basement of the church. There were several rooms on both sides with overhead doors to close on Sunday mornings for various classes.

There were school activities, Sunday school picnics, outings for the whole family at different parks. They kept very busy until they graduated from high school in the year 1950. This was the highlight of their youthful days. At last, twelve years of learning was coming to a close. They were so happy. In the fall, they would both attend college in Chicago, Illinois, at the Covenant North Park College. Josie took a nursing course at the Covenant Hospital and Charlie majored in business classes.

During breaks, they would return home to learn more about Sweden and Ireland. Eric promised he would take Charlie to Sweden the summer of his freshman year. He received a call from his mother in October of his first year that his childhood friend, Rudy, his beloved dog had died. He died quietly in his fourteenth year. Eric buried him in the backyard and put a cross over his grave.

Charlie mused over the years he and Rudy had romped together, visited Farmer Pete, met up with a naughty bird that caused him a great deal of harm. He remembered how Rudy would cuddle down at his feet at night in bed. He was his constant companion for years. He would tell him his troubles, and Rudy seemed like he understood his sadness and tears. He remembered the weeks he was missing after Halloween. He thought for sure he would never see him again. He had a picture of Rudy in his dorm room. That picture would be with him for life no matter where he went or lived. There would never be another friend like Rudy.

The next day, he told Josie at lunchtime in the cafeteria all about the death of his beloved dog. There were tears in his eyes as he related all the stories about his dog to his dear friend Josie. He held her hand and said, "Josie, I need you in my life now and forever. I don't have enough money for a ring right now, but will you promise to marry me after we graduate from college and nursing school?"

"Charlie!" Josie said with joy and admiration. "I would love to marry you. I couldn't think of a nicer man in all the world that I would like to spend the rest of my life with."

They held hands and talked of future plans. Then they decided that, for now, they would spend their time and efforts getting the education they needed to build a life for the future.

Summer vacation came and Eric and Charlie started making plans to tour Sweden and his dad's village of Bor Jo. They would sleep at the old homestead where his dad was raised. On the nineteenth of June, they flew out of Chicago to Stockholm, Sweden, where his cousin, Hans Olson, met them at the airport. They motored from there to the homestead and arrived at ten o'clock night. It was still daylight outside because they lived so close to the Arctic Circle. The sun wouldn't set until after two o'clock in the morning. The next morning, Rune Backman prepared breakfast for them. He couldn't understand a word of English so Charlie didn't know what he was saying, but Eric did and translated the Swedish to English and the English to Swedish the whole time he was there. The home was over 125 years old and had been remodeled several times during past years. It was quite modern looking now. The old wood range was gone, but the weaving loom was still there up in the attic.

The house was built on the edge of the woods. A huge rock was in the yard outside. It had been there ever since the house was built. In the forest behind, there were lingon berries growing. Rune had picked some of them to be served on Swedish pancakes that morning. Tomorrow was Midsummers Day with all kinds of festivities to follow.

This day was celebrated all over Sweden. If you lived in Stockholm, the capital of Sweden, you would not be going to work that day. Everyone would go to the countryside for that celebration. Most celebrations would take place at the church. Everyone would have Swedish pancakes that morning

In the morning, little girls with their mothers would go out and pick pretty wildflowers and form them into garlands to wear around their heads. This would mean that summer was here in full force and the flowers were now in bloom.

The family would go to the church cemeteries and place flowers on the graves of the loved one. A large pole had been decorated and raised in the church yard with streamers to hang on to and boys and girls would circle around the pole with a streamer in hand. All were glad the long, cold winter had come to an end, for during the winter, the days were dark most of the day.

The only cheerful time during this time was the celebration of Christmas with the oldest girl in the family dressed as

Santa Lucia with flowers on her head. She would serve the family hot tea and Swedish coffee cake.

At two o'clock, the Midsummer Festival would be held with Swedish folk dancing and Swedish folk music. People would eat all the goodies every family brought and drink lots of coffee and other beverages. Charlie was really having a good time celebrating with all his Swedish relatives. He thought they were all pretty special, especially Rune who was so glad to meet his American cousins before he died. He was eighty-six years old.

Rune had a green house in his front yard and spent springtime cultivating the plants he had started to plant when the frost season was over. He showed Charlie the shed where his grandfather had made horseshoes for all the local farmers. He had many tools in this shed.

In the evening, all the families would gather for the Midsummer Feast. This would include korve (Swedish potato sausage), krupe kraka (potato dumplings), Swedish coffee kakas, vegetables (Swedish brown beans), stuffed cabbage, salads, and desserts. What a wonderful feast, Charlie thought. He was so glad to be here for this awesome celebration.

The evening would be spent talking, laughing, and young folks playing games outside. Charlie went for a walk through the forest. Here in the fall, his cousin, Hans, would hunt moose. They have moose accidents in Sweden. There was an abundance of moose in the forest behind the old homestead.

When Charlie went to bed that night at 11:00, there were no moon or stars in the sky. It was still light outside. He slept in the attic next to the weaving loom and pictured his grandmother weaving rugs there. Now there were electric lights, but in those days, there were lanterns and candles.

The next morning, he awoke with the smell of coffee and bacon permeating the air. He got dressed and sat at the table while Rune talked of the olden days when lumbermen went off to the woods to cut trees for timber and others went to sawmills to cut logs for homes and outbuildings. They talked of farmers getting together in the fall to help each other bring in the crops. The women would make lunch for the gang and the young folk would play and romp outside.

They would take out hay wagons in the summer and rake hay into piles. Then they would take their pitchforks and load the hay wagons to bring to the barns where they, once again, would use pitchforks to load the hay into the haylofts. This was hard, tedious work. They went through lots of coffee on these special days.

They had been invited over to Ole Backman's house for lunch. It was a ten-mile drive from Ole's place. They went by the huge farm where Anna and Per Stordahl had met many years ago. Charlie had the chance of a lifetime of sitting in the pew where his grandparents sat when they attended church.

Ole and Anna Backman lived in a very nice modern white-framed home. They had the joy of dining outside and talked hours on end after eating about their heritage and where they grew up at children in Bor Jo. They went for a ride through the Swedish country side and viewed the beautiful lake that was situated behind the church where they celebrated midsummer. People in Sweden went to church when they were baptized as infants, when they went to confirmation, when they got married, and when they were buried. In the vestibule, there were pictures of all the pastors who ever served a church there. Charlie saw the pastor that was there when his grandfather attended church.

They spent the evening at Rune's daughter's home where his cousin Hans had spent his childhood. This home was right next to Rune's place.

During the next few days, they went for rides through the forest, visited the homes of other relatives. They saw the town where his grandmother had been raised and the houses of her two brothers that never married. The homes were painted a deep maroon color with a tile roof. Most of the homes in Sweden were white-framed with red tile roofs. There was a big family reunion dinner at a restaurant atop a mountain where the view of Sweden was magnificent. The dinner was delicious and the relatives talked and dined with their American relatives for the last time.

The next day, they were taken back to Stockholm to spend the night before they went back home. They went on a boat ride under bridges of various islands surrounding Stockholm. They saw a Viking boat and heard tales of the Vikings. There was Viking mounds scattered here and there throughout Sweden.

When they got back, they went to the palace to watch the Changing of the Guards. It was quite interesting and the music was lovely. The palace was a real work of art. They were hoping to see the king, but that was not to be so they went to bed that night at a swank hotel, said good-bye to their Swedish cousin, and in the morning caught the plane back to the States. Charlie was thrilled that he could visit Sweden and would remember those days spent there for the rest of his life.

9

After arriving home, he called Josie and told her all about his Swedish expedition. Eric came in the back door with the Sunday paper and showed Charlie an article. Charlie read it with great interest. It was about another arrest in the murder of Farmer Pete. George Wainwright's father, Chester, was a noted real estate agent in the neighborhood. He wanted Pete's land to develop a housing complex on Littlefield. George learned of his father's plight and talked to his dad about it. They cooked up a scheme that involved his two buddies to do away with the farmer. They didn't ever expect to be caught. They were sorry about killing the dog, but it lunged at them and would have bit them severely.

"Well," said Charlie, "that makes more sense than Pete being killed because his farm smelled!"

Eric replied, "There was no one more generous and giving than Pete. Why, he gave his neighbors string beans, snap peas, corn, and potatoes. He was always available to help whenever there was a need."

"I really miss my buddy, Pete. He sure was good to me and Rudy. I learned a lot from that man, especially about sod houses with thatched roofs."

Eric replied, "The pioneers who moved out west had sod houses because the vast majority of land in Nebraska was open plains with no trees. My Uncle Sven Stordahl had a sod house with a thatched roof. His wife lost their first child and both were buried together in the Svea Dahl church cemetery in Brady, Nebraska. Then he moved to Michigan, married a Detroit girl, and lived on Monica for the rest of his life.

That afternoon, Josie came over and the two of them sat with Colleen at the dining room table while she finished her talk on Ireland. She opened her book on Ireland and showed them the cobblestone streets and some of the sod houses over there. Her homestead had a sod house and all the outbuildings were sod with white-washed walls. Someday, she would take Charlie there to see the old place where she grew up.

"Look here, Charlie, this is Dublin where Saint Patrick's Cathedral is. Isn't this a magnificent building, Charlie?" Colleen asked.

"Yes, Mom, and this picture shows a woman named Molly Malone with a cart. Who was she?" Charlie wanted to know.

"She was a famous local lady who sold shellfish, cockles, clams, and other seafood. She would go all over Dublin with her wares and people would look for her whenever she came to town to get her fresh seafood," Colleen replied. "In Bunratty, you'll find the beautiful cliffs of Moher along the sea shore. There are palm trees in Dublin and other cities so that shows the winters are not severe in Ireland. That means that when the green grass grows, it stays for a long, long time."

She continued, "In Killarney, you can see shows at the local pub and visit the another castle in a small town outside the city. In Killarney, you can rent a jaunting car and ride around the National Park. It is a small cart with large rear tires that hold six people and is pulled by a horse. It's a lot of fun to ride. You would love it, Josie."

"There is another castle in Blarney and most folks who visit will kiss the Blarney Stone which is very hard to do. Someone holds you down while on your back and you lean way back to do this. But you always go away pleased because you endured this great feat and now good luck is supposed to follow you. In Kilkenny, you can walk through this large medieval city and see how they lived during those times. You will have to do it yourself to appreciate that era and be ever thankful that those days have passed."

"You can't leave Ireland without visiting beautiful Galway Bay near Connermara. There are many Irish songs that depict places and events. I have a book of Irish songs that I will give you, Josie. You and Charlie can sing them whenever you have the chance," Colleen exclaimed as she finished her dialogue on Ireland.

Josie took the book and looked through all the songs of Ireland. Some of them she knew. Charlie and Josie would go to Josie's house and sit down at the piano and Josie would play and they would both sing songs that made Josie grow more fond of her homeland and long to visit there some day. She and Charlie sang in the North Park Choir. She had a beautiful alto voice and Charlie sang tenor. They loved to sing together and would go to church on Sunday and very often would sing a special song for the Morning Worship hour at the Covenant Church. Charlie loved Josie dearly and looked forward to the day when they would be married and start a life together. He still hadn't given her an engagement ring so he talked the situation over with his mom and dad. He was hoping they would lend him the money to buy her the ring.

Then Eric said, "Charlie, I have the ring my father gave to my mother before they were married. It has a small diamond, but I would be very happy to have my future daughter-in-law wear my mother's ring. It would mean a lot to me. Just a sec, I will go and get it for you and you can decide whether or not it will be the ring for Josie. Your mother and I love this girl and believe you have made the right choice in selecting her as your future bride."

In a few minutes, Eric came back with a small well-worn box that housed this precious ring. He showed it to Charlie and he was delighted. He hugged his dad in appreciation and could hardly wait to drive to Josie's to give her this beautiful ring his grandmother wore until the day of her death.

It was a twenty-minute drive to Josie's. He just knew she would love it as much as his grandmother loved it. He drove up to her house and asked her to come sit on the front porch swing where they had spent so many endearing hours together. She sat by his side and he put his arm around her shoulder, holding her close. He pulled out the little box and, once again, proposed to her.

She, again, said yes, and he slipped the ring on her finger.

She shed a tear of joy and told Charlie it was so precious, she just loved it.

They sat there most of the afternoon talking about Farmer Pete, Rudy, his trip to Sweden, and hopefully, there would be a trip to Ireland some day to view all the beauty of that country. Her parents called them in for a late supper and the four of them talked of all the current events going on in Detroit. How things were booming after the war. The country was at peace and prosperity was there for most folks to enjoy.

10

Charlie got a part-time job at the drugstore on Tireman and Terry Street as a soda jerk and ice-cream sundae maker. It was fun and business was good. Once in a while, he would bring home ice cream in a bulk container and fill it himself with his mother's favorite flavor.

The family would go on picnics at Rough Park and Josie's family would accompany them. The two families were becoming close knit and bonded well together. There was a lot of talk about future plans and local and national events. They were all thankful that the war was over, Poland was freed, but Germany was divided and the Germans wanted to be united again. They had been through so much as a country. They also talked of the new vaccine for polio. Eric and Colleen wished it had been discovered before their baby girl contracted it and they had to lay her to rest at Evergreen Cemetery. Everyone in Detroit was thankful to Jonas Salk who had discovered it.

The summer months faded away, and once again, Charlie packed up and went back to college. He was very thankful for the job he got in the cafeteria where he would help cook and prepare meals for the day. He even had free meals because he worked there. Then there was choir practice, homework, etc.

At Christmas break of his senior year, Charlie got a phone call from his mother, Colleen. "Charlie, something dreadful happened to your father this afternoon. On his way home from work, his car slid on some black ice and careened into a tree. He was killed instantly. Can you come home as soon as possible? I really need you now." She was weeping as she talked and ended the conversation with deep, penetrating sobs.

Charlie lay on his bed and cried himself to sleep. He awoke early the next morning and thought he had had a nightmare. It really couldn't be true that his father, whom he loved so dearly, was gone. He mused on these thoughts for a long time. Then he dressed, went to the cafeteria, and fixed breakfast for his fellow classmates, wiping away tears as the morning progressed. He then went to the dean of the dorm and got permission to go home for the funeral and Christmas break. What a Christmas that would be. Just him and his mother!

Josie was now home for the break so she went with Charlie and his mother to make funeral arrangements. It would be held the Friday before Christmas at the church with the ladies furnishing the luncheon.

They would not put up a tree this Christmas, but he and his mom would go to the Stordahls for Christmas to help them alleviate the sadness that had settled upon the family. Colleen helped her mother-in-law, Ruth Stordahl, with the dinner. There were fifteen around the table. Most sat in silence as the meal was served. Some of the younger children talked and helped make happiness out of sadness. After all, Christmas was for the children, although the adults knew the real reason for Christmas and God had to see his own son die a cruel death that was senseless so that we would have Christianity today.

They gathered in the front room and Josie and Charlie led in a few Christmas carols. Then they opened their presents. Charlie received a new shirt, socks, and pants to match for school. Colleen received two new aprons, a flannel nightgown, and pearls. Josie received a new blouse and slip. They visited for several hours and went home rather tired. If only Eric could have been there, it would have been perfect, but he was in a better place now. Heaven became a real place now with Betty and Eric waiting for them to join them in that wonderful place that knew no pain, sorrow, or sickness.

Charlie and Josie went back to Chicago after the New Year had dawned. Hopefully, this one would be one that would heal their sorrow and bring some kind of hope and joy in their lives.

The months seem to fly by and another summer came. They had one more year to go before graduation and all the hoopla set in for that big event. In June 1954, they graduated with honors and received their diplomas.

They headed back to Detroit to spend a new life as graduates and make plans for their future. A wedding date had to be set, a home had to be established, a job had to be in the offing. Lots of decisions had to be made. It would mean careful planning and thinking that would affect the rest of their lives. They decided to look first for employment and then discuss what would lie ahead. What about Colleen, Charlie's mother? She was talking about going back to Ireland.

So with all this in mind, they decided to take one step at a time to make sure they were doing the right thing and that their plans would make sense.

Charlie stayed at home with his mother, who really appreciated his company. It had been so lonely since Eric died. Charlie and his mom got along really well together. Now he decided to go to the Burroughs Business School for some advice on employment. A date was set for the third Monday in June. Charlie began praying every day for guidance. He wanted a job where he felt comfortable and one he could perform with satisfaction.

Charlie went into the office at Burroughs and waited until he was called in for an interview. He only waited for around fifteen minutes when he was ushered into the main office. The manager asked many questions about his business background and Charlie answered as best as he knew how. Then he was told that a corporation named Mardigan was hiring a new accountant. It was located on Tireman and Whitcomb, which was only a few blocks from where he lived.

He went for an interview at Mardigan's with Burroughs backing him up. The manager seemed well-pleased with Charlie and hired him right then and there. He went to work the first week in July and was very thankful that he had gotten employed so quickly.

Josie had no problem at all getting employed. She went right away to Sinai Hospital not too far from where she lived and began working the Monday after they returned from graduating in Chicago. So now with both of them settled in new occupations, they could get together and make future plans for their wedding.

11

Charlie was introduced to all the office staff at Mardigan's. He was especially intrigued with a young black man named Kene Carver. He was a great-great-grandson of George Washington Carver (the inventor of all the peanut products.) They would have lunch together every day. Kene was a graduate of Burroughs Business School and was a very mentally sharp young man.

He invited Kene over quite frequently to have supper with him and his mom. These conversations were long and sometimes quite jovial for Kene had a sharp sense of humor and would make Colleen laugh a lot. She loved these times that Charlie invited him over to share a meal.

Whenever Josie worked the afternoon shift at Sinai, Kene and Charlie would go bowling or play tennis at McKenzie High School. Most often, they would take a swim in the pool for it was open evenings for the public to use. Kene enjoyed these times with Charlie. They were getting to be best friends. They could joke and compete and still be friends.

Kene had a small two-bedroom apartment near Tireman and Greenfield. He told Charlie about the time he stood on Greenfield and Joy Road and witnessed the funeral procession of Henry Ford who was buried on an estate on Joy Road not far from Tireman. He would never forget that day. He was a witness to the final leg of Henry Ford's journey as he saw this great event transpire.

As Kene and Charlie continued working together, they became known for the way they conducted themselves in the business world. They would play jokes on each other. One day, the office staff was laughing and laughing at Charlie. Kene had pasted a long tail on Charlie's back made up of masking tape. The following day, Kene found a bag on his desk all taped up, and when he opened it, a clown jumped out at him. The office staff laughed at all these practical jokes and began watching for the next one and who the culprit would be to spring the next incident.

Charlie talked a lot about Kene to Josie and told her that he really would like Kene to be his best man at their wedding. They decided to set the date for May 30 when the green grass grows in Detroit. It was Judy's birthday. This was fine with Josie.

Josie worked in the maternity ward at Sinai Hospital. It was in a black neighborhood so mostly young black ladies would come to have their babies born there, and Josie was the RN in charge. She worked long hours, mostly afternoons and midnights to complete her internship. It was hard work and a most responsible nursing occupation.

One night, around 10:00, a young woman came in from the Salvation Army Home for Unwed Mothers. This became a real challenge for Josie as the young girl had decided to put her baby up for adoption. She was single. Her boyfriend had deserted her and wanted nothing to do with the child he had fathered. She asked the young lady a lot of questions. She was told her name was Trina Sloyan. Her mother and father had removed her from their home. They were embarrassed to have a pregnant unwed mother in their home.

Trina was only seventeen and had to quit school. She was humiliated over her pregnant condition. She thought she was in love, but her boyfriend had used her for a sexual toy and never intended to marry her. So now, she was in Josie's care and became a real challenge for this girl embarking on her new role in life. Hour after hour went by. Josie consulted with the doctor assigned to her case. She told him Trina was suffering from back labor and began to tire from all the contractions while nothing seemed to be happening to bring about this birth.

Dr. Richardson told Josie to come back in two hours and they would talk over the matter. He seemed to think that things were progressing, even though not much seemed to happen. Trina had dilated to five centimeters, and he thought she was just going to have a longer labor because this was her first baby.

Trina had no sedative whatever. She felt she deserved all this pain because she caused her parents so much heartache. She bravely endured the pain and only moaned slightly although Josie saw she was really in distress. Finally after two more hours, she consulted with Dr. Richardson and he decided to do an operation on Trina and take the baby abdominally. The nurses came with the cart and helped her onto it and took her to the operation room and prepared her for surgery.

No one waited for the baby to be born out in the hallway. Trina was all alone for this blessed event with only Josie and the doctor there to deliver the infant.

Around 5:00 in the morning, Trina brought forth her first baby, a seven-pound baby girl. The cord was wrapped around the infant's neck, which was why the labor had been so long and tedious. Josie and another nurse worked on the baby for twenty minutes. Finally, the breathing became regular and the heart beat strong. Trina was brought back into her room, assured that the tiny baby would be all right.

Josie left an hour later and went home to tell Charlie about all that had happened. She told him that Trina was going to give the baby up for adoption, but she was going to try and talk her out of it when she went to work that night. She had worked overtime and lay down for a long sleep.

Charlie went to work and told Kene all about Trina and the baby. They both tried to figure out how they could help Trina so she could keep her baby. She had no job or babysitter. She had no place to stay. There weren't any baby clothes. All day long, they pondered the situation, looking for a solution.

Josie went to work that night. Trina wasn't sleeping. She had slept so much during the day, resting from the birthing ordeal. Now she was wide awake so Josie took advantage of the situation and sat down to talk. She found out from Trina that she hadn't even held her baby yet. She was advised that it wouldn't be wise when she was going to give up her rights to the child.

"Trina," Josie looked deep into her eyes and said, "please don't give her away. I saw her and she is beautiful. You know, Trina, no one can love that baby like her own mother. I know you have nowhere to go. No one to help you, no baby clothes or crib or any baby furniture, but Charlie and I are working on your problem and we will find the answers for you. Do not be concerned, it will all work out, just wait and see and have faith in us and God to help you. I want you to go to sleep for a while, then think things over, and we will talk it over."

"My mind is pretty much made up," Trina responded.

She had a tear or two in her eyes. It was quite evident that she was really concerned. She told Josie that at one o'clock the next day, the lawyer would be coming to have her sign away her rights to the baby.

12

Trina slept all night while the nurses tended to her infant. Toward morning, she had a dream. She held her baby in her arms and rocked her gently. The lawyer came into her room with papers to sign. She trembled and hung tightly to the baby. She was deeply troubled. The lawyer handed her papers to sign. She was hesitant. She sighed deep breaths and looked at her baby again. Then she picked up the pen and was going to sign the papers when she woke up, startled. The dream seemed so real. Josie entered her room half an hour before she would leave to go home.

Trina was crying. "Josie, I can't do it. I dreamed I held my baby and it seemed so right. I remember everything you told me. I am my daughter's mother. I am the one responsible for her. With your help, I know I can make it."

"I am going to bring the baby to you, Trina. I have a camera. I want to take a picture and show to Charlie and Kene."

"Who is Kene?" Trina wanted to know.

"He is a young black man that works with Charlie. He is five years older than you and is a wonderful person. I will invite him to come here with Charlie and introduce you to him. He is very interested in helping you get back on your feet."

Josie went out of the room and came back holding the baby in her arms for Trina to see. It was rather noisy in the maternity ward. The entire group of new mothers were talking about their babies, relating circumstances regarding their families and how they would cope with their new little ones. She put the baby into Trina's arms.

The baby was awake and alert and seemed to be looking right into Trina's eyes. In that moment, she fell in love with her daughter and a smile lit up her face. It glowed with happiness over being this child's mother. What a warm feeling came over Josie. It was more than she expected. A real answer to prayer.

Josie told her of the dream she had, and how, when she awoke, she knew she couldn't give up her little one.

Charlie was at work with Kene and they discussed, at length, Trina's situation.

"Charlie, my apartment isn't very big, but it has two small bedrooms. Trina could have one of them. I would have to get some chests of drawers at the Salvation Army Thrift Store. It's only a couple of blocks from where I live. Come with me after work and let's see what we can find to tide everything over until things begin to lie in place. At least, we can get started on the problem and take it all in stride to get everything settled."

Kene had a pickup truck so there was room to put the furniture or whatever they decided on in the back of the truck. So after work that day, Charlie followed Kene to the store. Now mind you, Kene had never seen Trina. He had no idea what she was like or what he was getting into. All he knew was that here was a person in desperate need and he just had to make himself available to help her. Kene, like Charlie, had no siblings. They were both the only child in the family. Would he be able to share his apartment with a complete stranger? There would be a crying baby, and goodness only knew what else would go into this new life he was now planning. Besides, he was a single man. How would others look at this living arrangement?

They spent two hours there picking out all the things needed for Trina and the new baby. They decided to have the manager set aside the different items until they knew for sure that this is what Trina would want for herself and baby daughter.

Charlie went home and Josie had just gotten up from her sleep after working all night. He told her of his and Kene's plans for Trina and the baby. After supper, they decided to pick up Kene and go visit Trina at the hospital.

It was seven o'clock when they went into Trina's room in the maternity ward. They found out that Trina had sent the lawyer away without signing the papers. She decided to name the baby Josephine Marie after her newfound friend, Josie. They all talked a long time about the future for Trina and the baby. After all was said and done, Trina decided she would go to Kene's apartment and live there until she got back on her feet and decided what she would do about her future. She would stay two more days at the hospital and then Kene would pick her up. In the meantime, Josie would look for baby things that were needed. Josie was so happy! At last, Trina had something to look forward to and she and Charlie would help her with whatever would transpire next.

On the fifteenth of July, Kene and Trina moved the new family into the apartment on Tireman. The small bedroom held a single bed, two chests of drawers, a table to bathe the baby and hold diapers on a ledge underneath the table. A bassinet stood near the bed and there was a small storage unit for baby clothes nearby. In the kitchen, there were many baby items that would be needed for feeding the child. Charlie and

Josie stayed for a while, talking, and just being helpful to get things off to a good start.

The baby was fed and put to bed. Trina said she was a good baby, only eating and sleeping and crying whenever she was given a bath. Charlie and Josie said good-bye and planned on bringing supper over there the following day. Josie went to work that night with a big burden taken off her shoulders. She really felt that this was going to work, and so with a sigh of relief, she put in her eight hours a very happy nurse.

The next morning, Charlie went into the living room and stood by his father's picture on the wall. He looked at his dad and said, "Thanks, Dad, I am the man I am today because of you. You always had time for me. You taught me how to play catch, pitch, and bat the baseballs. You helped form a team for me to play on. You were our coach. You encouraged us. You taught me patience and kindness. I will never forget how you walked with me all over the neighborhood looking for my puppy, Rudy. When the big bird tore his cheek and his talons punctured his back, you took me and my Rudy to the vet's. I hope and pray I will be the kind of dad to my kids that you were to me."

The very least he could do for his father was to take good care of his mother and see that she had a good life ahead for her. He loved his mom and counted it a privilege to have her in his care.

The next evening, Charlie and Josie took Kene and Trina for a ride to their old neighborhood. On the street where they had lived, Farmer Pete's house had been torn down with all the outbuildings gone. The hill in back where he and Rudy had sat with the farmer had been leveled. He, in his mind's eye, had gone back through time and he pictured the three of them together, talking on that little hill. He remembered the stories about Poland and the big Polish supper they had with the farmer's family. Charlie had tears in his eyes over that fond memory.

Now the farm was all parceled out into housing lots. A sign was on one of the lots stating "House for Sale, O'Shannon, Real Estate Agent."

"Too bad, Farmer Pete, I never shall forget you."

13

There were very few polio cases in Detroit since Jonas Salk invented the polio vaccine for which most residents were very grateful. If only it had been available a few years ago, little Judy Elizabeth would still be alive. But thanks be to God, many other lives would be spared.

Kene and Trina had grown accustomed to living together in close quarters. Kene became very fond of Trina and baby Josie. One day, as they were having breakfast in late September, Kene looked fondly at Trina and remarked with a strong, loving, compassionate tone, "Trina, I have come to love you and that adorable baby girl of yours. I would, very much, like to spend the rest of my life with you as my wife.

Will you marry me?" There was a moment of silence as Trina thought over this proposal of marriage.

"Kene, you have been so good to me. I feel so unworthy of your love. You know my background, how can you love someone who has made so many mistakes and made such a mess out of her life as me?"

Kene held out his hand and clasped hers in his. "When God forgives, He forgets. I live in love and forgiveness as all of us should. We belong together. Don't feel unworthy or guilty. It's all in the past. We can have a wonderful future ahead of us. I just feel with all my heart and soul that you and I are meant for each other."

With that said, Trina told Kene that she would marry him. Trina was small of stature but big of heart. Kene was around five foot seven inches tall. He was a very nice-looking young man with dimples on both cheeks. He wore his hair extremely short and Trina's hair was close-cropped. She wore a different color ribbon in her hair every day.

They began to make wedding plans for Thanksgiving Day and decided to ask Charlie and Josie to stand up for them to witness the ceremony. It would be just the four of them as neither one of them had families in the Detroit area. They invited the Stordahls over for supper the next evening and shared the good news with them. They had a wonderful time sharing and laughing together, making plans for the future of Kene and Trina.

Many changes were occurring in Detroit. There had been race riots in the forties. The unions at the car companies had initiated strikes to help their workers gain more money and benefits.

Laws were passed so that employers could no longer refuse to hire someone due to their race, color, or religious affiliations. These laws were new and many people didn't want to see them enforced. Some white people were moving out of the city because black people were moving into their neighborhoods. High schools now had black and whites attending. Restaurants had a very hard time with these new rules. One restaurant at one of the malls fired a black bus boy because he was found dancing with a white girl during lunch in the break area.

When Kene and Trina showed up at church with Charlie and Josie, some of the members were appalled and whispered behind their backs about what was happening in their church. This was when Charlie appeared before the church board and told them he would take out his membership if this continued. So the church board members prayed and decided that they had a place here that was the House of God and God created all mankind. America had become the melting pot of nations and people of all sorts of backgrounds. They must, as a church, respect all nationalities and make everyone feel welcome.

Charlie and Josie never told Kene and Trina about this situation. From then on, all the people welcomed them and enjoyed watching little Josie grow up in their church.

That afternoon at Charlie's house, they sat down and discussed their wedding plans. Of course, Kene and Trina would be their maid of honor and best man at their wedding.

"Now, Charlie," Kene exclaimed, "when are you two getting married?"

Charlie looked at both of them and spoke, "My dad, bless his soul, always told me of future events in my life that would happen when the green grass grows. So Josie and I are getting married when the green grass grows on May 30, which is the birthday of my sister, Judy. I think she will look down from heaven and be glad that we included her memory in our plans. We will be married at the Covenant Church and Pastor Clemmens will officiate."

Josie told them that she bought her gown at a bridal store on Grand River Avenue and West Grand Boulevard. She paid a whopping $25 for it. She wanted Trina to go there and pick out her gown for the wedding. Josie wanted her to be dressed in a long chiffon blue gown. The bridal party would be small and the ladies of the church will be asked to serve the luncheon that will be fixed by Charlie's mother. She would also bake their wedding cake.

The days seemed to pass faster than ever. Thanksgiving Day came and was held at Coleen's house. They had stopped going to Grandpa and Grandma Stordahl's house as everyone was getting married, having children, and wanting to have their own families together at holidays. They asked Pastor Clemmens to come, and after a wonderful tasty dinner with turkey and all the trimmings, the little wedding of Kene and Trina took place.

They rejoiced together and cut the wedding cake Colleen had made. It was three layers high with a bride and groom at the top. She had made red roses and placed them neatly all over the frosting. What a wonderful way to climax the Thanksgiving feast. Colleen said she would take care of baby Josie while they went on a weekend honeymoon. Josie had played the wedding march on the piano and she and Charlie sang "I Love You Truly" for the bride and groom.

Kene and Trina left for their honeymoon. Charlie and Josie stayed with Colleen and enjoyed the antics of baby Josie. She was getting so big and cuter every day. It seemed the baby was always trying to do new things. She was almost six months old and could sit up by herself. She smiled at them all the time they were in her presence. Josie was so glad that she talked Trina into keeping her baby. She was so happy that Kene accepted her into his life and now they had made a commitment to each other for the rest of their lives. This year, she and Charlie had a lot to be thankful for. Next year would be their time and they were having a lot of fun preparing for that nuptial event in their life's journey.

New Year's Eve found the four of them together again, playing games like Parcheesi. They watched the ball come down in Times Square on their new television set while holding hands and wishing each other a happy new year. Television was rather new to the residents of Detroit, but they were delighted to watch all the new shows such as *I Love Lucy*, *First Nighter*, *Bob Hope, Frank Sinatra, Dean Martin, and Jerry Lewis*, *Inner Sanctum*, etc.

14

The days in January were cold and snowy. The Stordahls listened to the news every morning to find out driving conditions. Detroit was building freeways all over Detroit to help with the traffic problems here and there. Colleen still took the bus to Hudson's in downtown Detroit. She liked to go to Sander's for a hot fudge sundae and once in a while to the Vernors plant where she got a glass of Vernors blended with ice cream for a special treat. In January, there were White Sales all over Detroit and things that weren't sold for Christmas were marked down 50 percent.

Charlie and Josie began to pick out wedding invitations for relatives outside of Detroit. They would announce their wedding in the church bulletin. In March, there was a bridal shower for Josie in the Church Fellowship Hall. There were forty-five women present and many gifts were received and enjoyed by Charlie and Josie. She registered her name at Hudson's and other stores so people could get an idea of what to give them for wedding presents. Mardigan's, where Charlie was employed, gave him a large roaster oven for which he was very grateful. The employees there told him they wouldn't attend the wedding because no alcohol would be available for consumption.

When the green grass grows in May, Josie walked down the aisle of the Covenant Church. Her uncle gave her away in marriage for her parents were both dead. Around 400 people attended the reception in the Fellowship Hall and really enjoyed Colleen's wedding cake that she baked for the joyous occasion. After the wedding, Charlie and Josie drove to Niagara Falls on their honeymoon.

They were surprised at how large and beautiful the falls were. They visited the gift shops and bought several items to remember this special time—their honeymoon. After three days, they headed back home to begin their marriage together. They bought a home on Marlowe, not far from Colleen so they could be there whenever she needed them. It had a large kitchen, small dining area, medium-sized living room, a bath, and two bedrooms with rooms available in the attic, which needed to be finished off whenever they were needed.

In August of 1955, Colleen received a notification that she had inherited her parent's old homestead. Now she was faced with a decision on what to do concerning this situation since the homestead was in Ireland.

After several days of deliberating, it was decided that Colleen would move back to Ireland where she grew up. She would live on the outskirts of Donegal in the old homestead. She put the house up for sale, and when it was sold, she would auction off all the house furnishings. Charlie and Josie would choose the items that they would like, especially his father's tools, snow shovel, and garden equipment so that he and Josie would be able to do some gardening.

Some black people came and bought the house Charlie knew as his home territory. He didn't like to say good-bye to the house on Robson. He had good memories from there. He loved playing ball with his buddies and turning the hose on his comrades in the summer. He loved ice skating at the Parkman School ice rink. He didn't like good-byes and he would really miss his mom when she went back to Ireland.

On September 15, Colleen said good-bye to Charlie and Josie. She hugged them close, while tears filled her eyes. When would she see them again? How would life be in Ireland after all these years? Her cousins would probably all be married by now. Would there be television over there? Would she find a Christian church to go to? When she was a lass, they attended the Catholic church. Lots of questions went through her head. She just knew that Josie would be having young ones. Would she ever see them? Was this really the right thing for her to do?

She boarded the Ocean Liner at New York City and traveled over rough and calm waters. Each lap of the wave reminded her that she was to embark on a new way of living without her son to be there for her. He had truly been a good son. Never a cross word was uttered from his mouth. He was kind and understanding. She would miss his shoulder to lean on. Many tears were shed on the long voyage to Donegal.

On September 30, the boat moored at Dublin. When she got off, Uncle Jacob met her at the boat. He was in his early eighties. His hair was gray. Time was catching up with the old man. His steps were slow and she could tell he was bothered with arthritis. He gave her a gigantic hug and took her bags. He led her to a rickety old car that had seen its better days. She got in and they chatted and chatted until he drove into Donegal. It was just as she remembered. Some new things had transpired since she left, but they were for the best.

The cobblestone streets were gone. They were now made of cement. Some of the old buildings had been renovated. A few new shops were now part of the scene. Then they drove up the driveway to the old homestead. The walls were still whitewashed as well as the outbuildings. She would use money from the sale of her home in Detroit to make improvements.

She walked into the house. A new carpet lay on the living room floor. New cupboards were in the kitchen. The walls needed to have new plaster walls. She had her work cut out for her. It would take months to make this place habitable. It would be a great undertaking. What would she do with the outbuildings? After musing things over, she walked out to some of the buildings to see what was in them. There were wild cherry trees growing in front of her house. She supposed that winters had become milder; otherwise, they would never endure. The cherry trees were in full bloom and they scented the entire acreage. Such wonderful smells!

There was an old car in one of the buildings. The key was above the steering wheel on the blind above it. She put the key in the ignition and started up the car. There was half a tank of gas in the car. She decided to go to the local grocery store and stock up on some much needed items. The refrigerator in the kitchen was empty. The door was left open so as to prevent mold on the interior.

She drove to O' Donavan's store, and what did she know, but that skinny Katie was still working there. Katie remembered her and they talked at length about what was taking place in Donegal. After an hour, Colleen had purchased all she wanted to buy and headed for home where she put away all her groceries. Colleen's red hair was now graying at the temples. She was fifty-five years old. This was her new adventure in life. She hoped she was up to the challenge.

She spent hours looking through catalogues and going to hardware stores and visiting furniture stores to purchase items she needed to fix up the old homestead. After days of hammering, washing, painting, and buying items, the old homestead began to take on new looks. Elmer Finnigan sure did a nice job putting up new plaster board and his brother, Liam, was making the old outbuildings look really modern and useful. One of the buildings would house things needed for gardening and used to keep the lawn mowed. Two of the buildings remained empty to be filled with useful things as needed. This renovation had been fun and pleasing to Colleen when she saw the end result. But she missed Charlie and Josie!

As time went on, Colleen knew she needed an income of some kind. All the inheritance money had been spent as well as most of the money from selling the house in Detroit. She heard of a shop on Fifth Street that was empty and up for sale. She inquired of the owner the details of moving in and renting the building for a Bake and Sew Shop. The owner assured her that he would work with her to make the business profitable and robust. She had to purchase equipment and buy a sewing machine for the Sewing Room. There were a few tables there where patrons could sit down for coffee and donuts.

Soon, the place became a beehive of activity as the elderly liked to come in and spend time talking to each other over a fresh brewed cup of coffee. Everyone that came in seemed pleased with the baked goods they purchased. Colleen hoped it would be a thriving business. She loved the thought of making her livelihood in this manner.

In late November, she received a long overdue letter from Charlie. He told her that she was going to be a grandmother when the green grass grows in the spring. The date was early May. Josie found out in September that she was pregnant. Almost from the very beginning, she had morning sickness, which soon grew to be all-day sickness. Aromas nauseated her and even driving in a car would make her vomit. She spent most of the time stretched out on the couch sleeping. She was too tired to cook, clean, or do the laundry. When Charlie came home, he knew fixing supper was entirely up to him.

Charlie told his mother that Josie was pale and dehydrated from her sick pregnancy. After three months, the doctor told her that if the nausea didn't stop, he would have to terminate the pregnancy. Josie cried and he gave her some pills he thought would make her well again. She swallowed one pill and immediately it came up and left an awful taste in her mouth. Colleen was upset over this state of affairs and she went about her business in a worried state of mind.

15

Back home in Detroit, Charlie worried about his wife every day that he went to work. He began to pray for Josie every time he thought about how sick she was. Josie was losing weight. She had lost fifteen pounds, and when she went to buy maternity clothes, the medium sizes hung pretty loose and free, but she purchased them anyway. The trip to town to buy these clothes was very tedious. She had eaten a few soda crackers before she left home, hoping they would stay and settle her stomach. It seemed to work and she hurried home before the next wave of nausea set in.

She stopped at the corner drugstore and noticed that Coca-Cola was on sale at a bargain price so she bought a six-pack along with some milk of magnesia for nausea. Once she was home, she lay on the couch and took a long nap. When she awoke, she went to the kitchen and took one of the bottles of Coke. She drank it slowly as she did with water and liquids, hoping they would stay down.

She turned of the television and watched *As the World Turns*. Soon her head slumped back and she was asleep in the chair.

Josie awoke two hours later and soon noticed that she didn't feel nauseated. She went to the kitchen and drank another bottle of Coke. Wow! What a relief, the upset stomach was better. She got up and looked for something in the refrigerator to fix for supper. Charlie would be home in another hour. She made some chili from the hamburger she found and the smell didn't make her upset. She smiled broadly and did a little dance around the kitchen. At last, she found something that helped and she was so happy.

When Charlie came home from work, he found Josie in the kitchen setting the table for supper. The aroma of chili filled the air. He couldn't believe his eyes. Josie came and gave him a big hug. She told him of her newfound relief from nausea. He held her close and told her how glad he was. Maybe they could go for a ride and celebrate at Kene and Trina's house.

After the dishes were done, they motored over to Kene's and told him and his wife the good news. They had good news of their own to tell him. Trina was pregnant and expecting in late August. They seemed so happy. Little Josie was crawling around now. She was a beautiful little girl and brought so much happiness to this deserving couple who had made an impact upon their lives. Charlie didn't know what he would do without Kene's friendship.

When Charlie got back home, he wrote his mother about the great changes Josie had experienced and the new pregnancy for Kene and Trina. He knew the news would relieve her mind. He was glad everything was working out for her. He missed her so much. He wished she could be here when the little one arrived. It would make her so happy.

Three weeks later, Charlie got a letter from his mom. She told him that she was making leprechaun outfits for the big event in May when all of Ireland went leprechaun hunting. Boys and girls three and four years old would don the suits that had bright copper buttons and black belts around the waist. Their parents would hide them some place on the farms or in their backyards and the person who found the most leprechauns would receive a $50 grand prize from the Government of Ireland.

Parents would rehearse with their children what they should do and where they should hide. This was a lot of fun for families and brought lots of laughter as the hunt progressed. Colleen suggested that when their little ones were old enough, they should go to Ireland for this fun time.

Charlie let Josie read the letter and she was really interested in making this happen when their little one became of age to enter the great frolic.

The weeks passed and one day in late May, around suppertime, Josie told Charlie that she thought labor had begun. She started timing the pains and packed her little suitcase to take to the hospital. Charlie called the doctor and he told him that when the pains were ten minutes apart to call and make their way to Sinai Hospital. Josie had taken time off of work due to the difficult pregnancy so she was anxious to go and see her friends again that she worked with.

At eight o'clock, Charlie called Dr. Richardson and off they went to the hospital. The staff greeted Josie and welcomed her arrival. Seems like the baby knew better when to arrive and Charlie was all right with the fact that this was May 27 and not May 30. He guessed the baby knew better.

Josie was prepped to have the baby and the labor continued. Around midnight, the pains had increased enough so that she was taken into the delivery room.

Jean Bergstrom was the attending nurse and guided Josie into the functions of delivery while Charlie waited in the waiting room. Men were not encouraged to be with their wives in the 1950s. Charlie respected the privacy and patiently waited. Jean encouraged Josie to push and push and push. Josie, tired of this, was getting impatient with Jean, but she was told to continue.

"You don't want to be here all night, do you?"

Josie told her no and tried to comply even though she was getting exhausted with all the pushing. Jean went and got the doctor and he arrived shortly after being summoned. Long about six o'clock, a new little life entered the world: a baby girl, six pounds and seven ounces. She was nineteen inches long. The baby was a little small, but Josie had a trying pregnancy and was surprised the baby weighed that much.

They took Josie back to the maternity ward. Charlie had been told in the waiting room of the baby's arrival by Dr. Richardson. The baby was strong and healthy. There were no complications. He looked into the nursery and saw this tiny white baby in the midst of many black babies. Then he went to visit Josie, gave her a big hug and kiss. They decided to call her Deborah Jean. Deborah was a character in the Old Testament that was an outstanding judge in the days when most of the judges were men.

The nurse came in with little Debbie and they held her and gazed into her little face to see if they could tell which side of the family she looked like. She had black hair. Josie said, "I don't think she is Irish, but I love her anyway," and they both laughed.

In late August, Kene and Trina called and said that Kene Junior had made his appearance in the world. He was also born at Sinai Hospital so Charlie, Josie, and Debbie made their way to Sinai Hospital to see the newborn son of the

Carvers. He was a big baby, almost nine pounds and twenty-one inches long. Now Charlie had something to write and tell his mother.

Colleen had told Charlie about the leprechaun hunt and how the parents loved the little frocks Colleen had made for them. She seemed so happy there in Ireland, but she longed to see her new granddaughter.

16

The Carvers and the Stordahls had a lot of fun together watching their little ones grow up. Charlie would send his mother pictures of Debbie and little Kene and little Josie. They spent holidays together for most of the Stordahls had families of their own and would celebrate together. On the last Saturday of June, they would have a family reunion at one of the parks. This was their way of keeping in touch with each other and watching their families grow.

Josie found herself pregnant again the middle of July. This baby would be born the latter part of March the next year. Their two little ones would be about ten months apart. Colleen found out in August she was going to be grandmother again.

Life in Ireland seemed to be just great. She had hired a middle-aged woman named Cathleen to help her in the bakery department of her shop in Donegal. Cathy was a good worker and very friendly with the patrons who dined at the table in her shop. Colleen would love it if her son and family could afford a trip to Ireland.

One morning, a gentleman walked in whose name was Patrick O'Malley. He was about six feet tall with curly red hair and dimples on both cheeks. He was clean shaven and had just opened a barber shop a few doors down from the bakery and sewing Shop. He loved the crullers that Colleen fried and became a regular fan of her Irish stew. He would joke and kid around and make all the patrons laugh. He was so funny, Colleen thought.

One day, he asked Colleen to go with him to the town picnic where they celebrated the founding of Donegal each year. There were lots of games played and shoe tosses for ladies and pie-eating contests for the men. Pat had been the winner for the last two years. The ladies would make blueberry pie so it would really make a mess of their face when they were finished. Each contestant had one pie placed in front of him and the one to finish first would be the winner.

Pat put on a bib. He did this to keep his shirt clean from blueberry drippings. He was a messy eater. The gong was sounded and the men began eating their pies. Pat took a big bite, which was almost more than he could handle. Berries began dripping from his chin and onto the bib. It only took him ten minutes to gulp down the pie. Then he roared with laughter as he saw the faces of the other men who took part in the contest. Pat was declared the winner and Colleen brought him a wash cloth to clean off his face. The prize was $10. A reporter from the newspaper took his picture which would be printed in the paper that weekend.

Pat and Colleen feasted on the picnic fare. After the meal, several Irish musicians got up and sang some old Irish songs, "Danny Boy," "I Will Take You Home, Cathleen," "When Irish Eyes Are Smiling," etc. Colleen sang along with the musicians and soon everyone joined in on the singing. There was a beautiful sunset in Donegal that night and Pat walked Colleen to her home on the outskirts of town.

From then on, Pat and Colleen became a dating couple. Colleen felt such a joy in her heart. Things were working out quite well for her. Now she had a buddy she could talk to and spend time with. It made her lonely days now a thing of the past. Pat would be at the bakery shop for a morning break from his barber shop each day. The bakery became quite busy with new patrons all the time. Colleen found herself hiring another helper since business had picked up. She would feature specials for lunch and soon her shop was the talk of the town. Seemed like more and more people loved to have coffee and donuts there.

Colleen found out that Josie was pregnant again, so she began sewing things for the baby. She found herself making little boy's apparel. She didn't know why, but she just felt this baby would be a boy.

In the fall, Pat proposed marriage and she accepted. She wrote to Charlie that she was going to be married again in the spring, when the green grass grows. She told Charlie he should come to the wedding and give her away.

Charlie talked it over with Josie. They decided to save as much money as possible and go, but Colleen was doing so well that she offered to pay their way to Donegal. The baby should be born by then and she could see both of her little grandchildren. Charlie and Josie accepted her offer.

In March 1958, Timothy Paul was born. He wasn't quite seven pounds, and he was twenty inches long. The pregnancy and the birth went well. Charlie never realized how rewarding it could be to have little children dependent on him. Now he had a daughter and a son! Kene and Trina came to the hospital to see the new baby. He had fuzzy blond hair all over his head. Charlie thought he looked a lot like his father, Eric.

A week later, mother and son came home and Charlie sat down and wrote his mother all the particulars of the birth. He told her that Debbie seemed to love her new brother, but she was just a baby herself. She wasn't even walking yet. This proved to be a hindrance for Josie. It was hard to tend to a baby and lift a ten-month-old child.

When Tim was two months old, they boarded a plane for Donegal. Since the airplane had been invented and flown successfully by Orville and Wilbur Wright in the early 1900s, it became a really growing industry for the nation by the time the 1950s came around. The airplanes were successfully used during World War I and World War II. Everything that was possible was done to ensure the safety of the travelers on the plane. Charlie and Josie held hands when the plane took flight. The children were too young to know what was going on, but the parents were in awe with the entire flight. They took turns looking out the small window. The clouds below the plane looked like a soft, puffy, white blanket. They could see the ocean below once the cloud cover dispersed. It surely was an amazing time to be alive.

They arrived in Donegal in early May. The wedding was planned for May 15 in the Donegal Town Square. The Irish musicians that had been there for the town picnic were now playing at playing at Colleen and Pat's wedding.

Before the wedding, Charlie and Josie visited the bakery and sewing shop and were very impressed with all that had happened to Colleen since she moved back to Ireland. They loved what she had done with the house and outbuildings. They thought her car was unique and told her so.

Colleen took the Stordahls to many places and showed them what a great country Ireland was. She hoped their visit was all that they hoped it would be.

Charlie really liked Pat O'Malley and he told him so. He thanked him for taking such good care of Colleen and was thankful that he was going to marry his dear mother. The two men left the women and children. Charlie wanted to get to know Pat. Pat suggested they go to one of his favorite fishing holes. He provided Charlie with all the gear to go fishing and they spent an entire afternoon together fishing and talking. Charlie found Pat to be a very likable fellow. They brought back a few fish to cook for dinner that night and continued visiting until the moon was high in the night sky.

The wedding was very well attended. It appeared as if the whole town was there for this popular woman's wedding to Pat. Colleen had made all the food for the reception and ladies from the Catholic church helped serve the food and cleaned up afterward.

Pat and Colleen went on their honeymoon to Dublin. They took in all the Irish countryside and slept in one of the old castles there. Colleen was a very happy bride. Charlie and Josie and babies left the next day to go back to America, but Josie thought in her heart, "Charlie wants to move here!"

17

In late July of 1958, Charlie and Kene were at work at Mardigan's. They were talking in the break room eating lunch when Sam Mardigan entered and told them of a small yacht he wanted to sell. The three of them talked at length, and after twenty minutes or so, Charlie and Kene found themselves the new owners of *Destiny*. He and Kene would have to take out a small loan each to cover the expense, but the price was very affordable. Sam was really giving them a deal.

They knew they were in trouble for not consulting with their wives, but this boat would give them a lot of pleasure for many years. Each one would bring up the subject to their wives that evening. They both went home not knowing how this deal would go over with Josie and Trina.

Charlie entered his home and Josie greeted him, as usual, at the door. He immediately told her that he had something to talk over with her and so they sat at the kitchen table, and Josie poured her husband a fresh brewed cup of coffee.

"Josie, Kene and I have bought us a small yacht that sleeps four people. It has a small refrigerator and gas stove to cook on. It is moored at Grosse Pointe Farms where Sam Mardigan lives. We can use it on weekends and have a lot of fun sailing over the lakes and rivers around here. I know I should have talked it over with you, but it sounded like a good deal and I didn't want to pass up this great opportunity to buy the boat. Its name is *Destiny*. I think that was one of the reasons I really wanted to buy this boat," Charlie said. His eyes danced with excitement as he reached over to hold Josie's hand.

Josie replied with some consternation in her voice, "Yes, Charlie, you should have told me. That's why I married you. You seemed so open and honest and really came across as a man who would talk and confide in me, but I also can understand how you and Kene felt about the deal. Guys like boats, and when this deal arose, I guess you couldn't turn it down."

"Josie, that's why I married you," Charlie replied. "You always seem to know how I think and why I think certain things. I feel like a very lucky man to have a wife that understands me. I just hope Kene is having a captivating talk with Trina. She seems to be a very passionate, understanding person and she will always feel an obligation to Kene for marrying her and giving baby Josie a name and a father to help raise her."

Just then, the telephone rang and Charlie answered. After the conversation, he told Josie that Trina had agreed to the purchase. Now they could make many plans for outings with their newly bought boat.

The four of them met at Charlie's that weekend. They discussed at length the plans to go pick up *Destiny* the following weekend. They would bring bags of groceries and other things that would be needed on the boat. They would leave their little ones with Margery, a nurse at Sinai, who had offered to babysit whenever she was needed. How she would manage with four little ones would be a real exciting experience, but she loved the thought of having the opportunity. She had wanted children, but was not able to have them.

So on Friday after work, the four of them packed clothes and took the other staples they had bought, put them in the car, and took off for Grosse Pointe Woods. It took about forty-five minutes to make the drive to Sam's house. Once there, they lost no time in loading the boat which had a full tank of gas and was ready to go for its maiden voyage with the Carvers and Stordahls.

Josie and Trina had fun cooking supper together. They laughed and teased each other and could hardly wait for Kene and Charlie to taste the meal they had prepared. They ate and chatted about future outings on the boat. Each one suggested places they would like to go. Right now, they were headed for Lake Huron and would have their first night together sleeping on the boat.

Kene and Charlie took turns navigating the boat through the waters. Finally, they dropped anchor and settled in for the night. The next morning, they arose early, ready for another day to enjoy *Destiny*. Charlie fixed Swedish pancakes for breakfast with blueberries that Josie had canned. They all remarked how good they were. Kene made fun of the thin pancakes, teasing Charlie while the pancakes cooked. But after the first bite, he shut his mouth. They were delicious!

Late Saturday afternoon, the wind began to pick up. Dark clouds filled the sky. The waves went from choppy to big waves in a relatively short time. The ladies, alarmed, started putting things away so nothing would spill, but Kene assured them the boat could withstand the tempest. It was getting harder and harder to steer *Destiny*. Josie made some sandwiches that they ate on top deck so the men could navigate over the troubled waters.

The waves grew higher and higher. All four of them put on life preservers. The boat went up and down over the waves. The rain became very intense.

The men instructed the women to go down below and try and stay dry. But Josie and Trina insisted on staying top side. All four of them began to pray. The boat was filling with water as it was taking on more water with each plunge of the waves. The ladies began bailing out the water and fear began to settle into the very core of their being. They couldn't see land anywhere for the rain was pouring down on them. They kept on bailing out the water while *Destiny* was beginning to take on more water. Suddenly, one gigantic wave turned the boat on its side and threw them into the water.

The men encouraged the ladies to stick close to them and rely on their preservers to keep them above the water. They had no idea where they were. Land couldn't be spotted anywhere. They began to tread the water and tried to stay close together. Another hour and it would be dark. No one knew they were out here in this part of Lake Huron. They held hands with each other while their free hands sought to keep their preservers afloat.

The water was getting cold now after they had been capsized and had been marooned for the night. The rain let up, but they were very cold. Each one tried to spy out land in some direction. Finally, Kene said, "Look over there, isn't that a small island I see?"

They all looked and looked, when Josie agreed that it sure looked like a small island out on the lake. They began to swim their way to the speck in the water. Exercising gave them a little warmth. After two hours, they managed to walk ashore.

"Now what?" Josie exclaimed. "We have no matches to start a fire, the twigs on the sand are all wet, and we are freezing cold."

They sat down on the sand and huddled together to generate some warmth.

"I'm going to walk around and see what I can find on this little island," Charlie said.

He got up while the others remained huddled together. He walked along the shore of the island. He noticed what looked like a pathway, so he followed it. It led away from the shore toward the inland. Daylight wouldn't be with them for very much longer. He noticed a small hill ahead and walked to it. There on the other side of the hill was a small indentation about three feet deep. He peered down to see some dry twigs on the bottom. Like the good Boy Scout that he was, he began to rub the twigs together, and after some time, he got a spark or two to ignite the small pile of twigs. He went out and gathered more sticks and twigs together. There was a small cove of trees nearby, which helped protect more branches on the ground from being rain soaked.

He took some of the twigs and laid them close to the small fire until they dried enough to start burning. He kept doing this with small bunches until he got a good fire going. Then he ran down the pathway that led to the beach and got the rest of the gang and brought them to the fire. The men went out collecting more branches and twigs. It took a while. The ladies went out to see what they could find to eat. They were becoming very hungry. They sure missed the morning coffee! What they discovered, only ten feet away was a cave about ten feet deep. They had noticed some large rocks as they followed the hill. Just past the largest rock was an opening into the hill. The opening was about two feet wide and about four feet tall.

Josie shouted out, "Guys! Come here!"

The men came running. Trina pointed at the cave and said, "I think this might be a good place to spend the night. Can we move the fire?"

Charlie and Kene stooped down and entered into the cave with the women right behind them. They could all stand up once they were inside.

"Good eyes, ladies!" Charlie hugged Josie.

Kene stated, "This will be a great place to stay warm."

The two men set out and moved the fire to a place near the front of the cave. The women left to see about something to eat. The women hunted and hunted, but to no avail. There were a few birds up in the trees, but getting them caught was another problem. Then Trina spotted a turtle and grabbed it, taking it back to the small cave. There was no knife to kill it. Charlie took a large rock and whapped it on its head, then he threw it on top of the fire and after an hour, took it off. It cooked within the shell. They would tug on pieces of turtle, eating whatever they had managed to extricate, thankful for a little morsel of food.

After eating the small meal, they all tried to make themselves comfortable inside the small cave. Their combined body heat helped to stay warm. The men decided to take turns during the night to keep the fire burning. Charlie was the first one to go outside and fill the fire pit with the branches and sticks that had been collected and stocked near the fire. A few hours later, Kene awoke and tended the fire.

Morning dawned bright and sunny. The group of four stepped out of the cave and stood by the fire to stay warm while they discussed what to do. They decided to walk around the island and see if there might be some way of escaping and getting back to the main land. The whole island was a mile and a half in circumference. They came upon a small brook in the middle and helped themselves to laps of water. They could see land ahead of them. It looked like a larger island nearby and they wondered what the name of it was. There was some movement on that island, but they couldn't tell what it was.

Charlie pointed at it and said, "I think I could manage to swim over there, but there is no telling when I would return with help. You will just have to wait and keep yourselves busy until I return."

Kene replied, "Well, it could be that we will have to spend another cold night here. We will have to scrounge around for wood. Seems like we got most of it. If we ration it out, burning a little at a time, it could last until tomorrow morning."

Josie spoke up, "We will manage somehow. At least you know where we are, and you will do the best you can to get back to us. This is one adventure I wasn't counting on. I am so thankful we made it through that awful night of high waves and pelting rain. We could have died from hypothermia! Thankfully, we made it through the night and today will just be another adventure."

"This is one experience I shall never forget," Trina replied. With that Charlie, put on his life preserver and walked out in the lake until it became deep enough for him to swim. Before he left, they all wished him the very best and Josie gave him a big hug and kiss good-bye.

After plunging into the cold water, Charlie swam until he tired. Then he floated until he had rested awhile. He then began the final swim of the lake until he reached the island. After landing, he took off the preserver and hid it behind a tree not far from the sandy shore. He then began walking, following some tire tracks until he came to a road. After considering his options a spell, he turned right and began walking along the road.

He figured he had walked half a mile when he came to a small house on the right side of the road. He walked up and knocked on the door. No one seemed to be home, so he continued walking down the road.

Then he spied another home on the left some distance ahead. He was beginning to tire, but kept on anyway until he reached the house. He rang the bell, and after a minute or two, a gentleman answered. Charlie introduced himself to the man and told him of his plight and of the three he had left behind on the small island. The man told him his name was Henry Jones. After talking to each other for several minutes,

Henry told Charlie he owned a boat out in the storage shed and would get it in back of his truck. Charlie and Henry tugged and pushed the boat up a ramp to the truck until it was securely fastened down.

The time was twelve thirty in the afternoon, so he took Charlie into his kitchen, and his wife Ivy made some sandwiches and took some other goodies and packed them in a bag for the stranded people on the island. Ivy told Charlie he was on Green Island and the smaller island had no name and was uninhabited and was used by the locals for picnic purposes. They fed Charlie a lunch and he gobbled it down in no time at all.

Around three thirty in the afternoon, they arrived at the little island and some very happy, hungry people welcomed them with hugs. They ate the lunch prepared by Ivy, then boarded the boat and motored to Green Island where they spent the night at the Jones'.

Charlie called Sam Mardigan in the morning and he promised to meet them at the dock if they could get a boat to take them over. Kene and Charlie arranged for Henry to take them there, and on Sunday morning, around nine, they came to Grosse Pointe Farms. Four happy bedraggled people met Sam who welcomed them back home. Finally, they were back home, none the worse for the experiences they had just gone through.

18

A week later, Charlie woke from a very bad dream. He was trying to navigate his body through waves of water that kept tossing him up and down like a yo-yo. Rain was pelting down on him. Cries were coming from those surrounding him. They were helpless and hapless as the storm still surged over and around them. Then, he felt his body sinking below the waters of Lake Huron and he awoke with a start. He dreaded that nightmare that seemed to occur every night. Finally, he arose and went to the living room and sat in his easy chair which faced the picture of his father, Eric, hanging on the wall.

"Dad, it's so good to be back home from that awful ordeal out on the waters of Lake Huron. I wish these dreams would cease and peace would come to my mind again. Dad, thanks for all the lessons you taught me on patience and perseverance. Those lessons made me strong and very courageous. It seemed like those about me trusted me to be the one to lead them out of that awful predicament. This was how I trusted you. Thanks for teaching me good sportsmanship. Thanks for taking me to watch the Detroit Tigers play ball. Hank Greenberg, Rudy York, Dizzy Trout, what great ball players they were. Then you took me to watch the Lions, the Red Wings, the Pistons. All those teams are still doing great. They aren't in the play offs or anything, but the Red Wings have won the Stanley Cup a time or two. I remember the times we went to the zoo and rode the train around and watched the chimp, Joe Mendy, as he performed. The State Fair was always fun to go to. They made a big model of a cow out of butter, there were rides on the ferris wheel and the merry-go-round. We had hot dogs and pop. I miss you, Dad. I don't think you would like the way Detroit is going. More and more people moving to the suburbs. Remember when it took us seven hours to ride to Cheboygan to see Great-grandpa George Stordahl and Great-grandma Hilda Stordahl? If we had a flat tire, it would take us even longer. I loved visiting up there. They had wonderful Sunday school picnics out at Aloha. They played games just like we did here at our church picnics. There was a big barn in back where we would grab a rope and sail from one side of the hay mow to the other side. I had such good memories of childhood days. There have been a lot of changes here in Detroit, Dad. There are large two-lane roads that are called freeways. There are large shopping malls all over the city now. The one near us on Greenfield is called North Land. There is even a J. L. Hudson Store there. Josie is working part-time at Sinai now. When I come home from work, she goes there for four hours while I tend to the little ones. Debbie has red hair. She sure looks Irish. Mom says baby Tim is a Swede over and over. They are growing up so fast. The Sand Lot Ball Teams you started have now become Little League and that is making summer productive for a lot of boys sports wise. I get lots of letters from Mom in Donegal. She seems really happy in her new marriage. I really wouldn't mind moving there, Dad. A farm would be a wonderful place for my children to grow up on. Farm chores are good for kids. All the baby animals and chicks will teach then responsibility. Well, Dad, maybe some spring when the green grass grows, I will move my family to Donegal."

Charlie rose from the easy chair and went back to bed where he slept until the alarm clock went off. Some day, he decided, he would have this same talk with Josie that he had with Eric.

While Charlie was at work that day, Kene came over to him during the coffee break and sat down and looked at Charlie with a very serious countenance. "Oh, oh," Charlie thought.

"Something is very somber about something. I hope it's nothing too drastic."

He was quiet for a moment or two and then looked at Charlie, again with that serious expression, "Sam Mardigan called me into his office and told me that the boat was still covered by insurance and not to worry, there would be money for us to pay off the boat loan. He also told me that he was very pleased with my work performance and that he wanted to send me out of the city to Atlanta, Georgia, to work at the factory there as business manager. There would be a substantial raise in salary."

"Wow!" Charlie exclaimed, "I suppose that's a deal that you can't turn down, but I surely will miss my best friend and I know Josie will surely miss Trina, but you have to do what's right for your family. Sounds like a proposal you should really act on. When would you be leaving?"

"I will be leaving as soon as I can make all the arrangements. You have been the best thing that ever happened to me. I have my wife because of you and Josie. I have my church home because of you and Josie. We have had more good times than bad times. The worst being in that storm, but we are all the stronger in character and belief because of it. If we can live through something as awful as that, we can live through anything."

"Come over for supper this weekend and we will have a farewell meal and then Josie and I can help you pack up all your belongings and put them in the moving van."

"Okay, we will be there. Georgia is a long way from Michigan so I know we won't be seeing much of each other," Kene replied.

Josie was not too pleased with the news that Charlie shared with her that night, but she would go to the local grocery store and buy a pot roast to have for their farewell meal together.

Saturday came and the four of them settled down together at the table. They had spent the majority of the day hauling and packing furniture. Now it was time to sit down and enjoy a meal. Little Josie was in her high chair and little Debbie in another high chair. They played with their spoons to see who could make the most noise banging their plates. They would laugh and laugh the harder they banged the spoons. There was much discussion at the table over their past experiences together as families and what would lie ahead for the future. When the Carvers went home, all kinds of hugs were given, and in a few days, the little family was on its way to Georgia. Josie and Trina both shed tears as they left each other.

19

In 1960, Charlie sat down with Josie to have a long talk. Another daughter with red hair had been born the previous year. Debbie and Tim were now brother and sister to a new sibling. Debbie was in kindergarten and Tim was anxiously waiting for the day when he could start school. They loved playing in the big sandbox in back and running through the sprinkler in the summer time. With another baby, Josie decided to give up her job and become a full-time mother to her small brood.

"Josie, I have been doing a lot of thinking. Detroit isn't the same place that it was when I was growing up. There have been a lot of changes. Jobs are scarce. Factories are moving to other states, leaving gaps in the employment picture.

Schools are becoming unsafe. At some of the schools, there are armed guards patrolling the halls. There are a lot of robberies, murders, and it's just not safe for anyone to go out at night. What do you think about moving to Donegal? All of Mom's letters tell of what a wonderful place it is there. She needs help on the farm because she and her hubby are busy managing the bakery and sewing shop.

"They have expanded now and set up tables in the new area. They now serve lunches. Mom isn't young anymore and she says that she would like some help and maybe let us take over her business some day."

Josie could tell by the frown on Charlie's face that this matter was of great concern to him. Her red hair was showing a gray hair here and there, although she was still relatively young.

"Charlie, I share your concerns, but let's really think this through. I don't believe there is room enough in your mother's house for our growing family. Why not see if she could add on a room or two to or see if there is a farm nearby that we could move to?" Josie's eyebrows were raised as she looked deep into Charlie's eyes. She didn't want to make rash decisions, but she knew in her heart that Charlie wanted to move to Ireland ever since their visit.

Charlie replied, "I will write to Mother right away. It will take a week or so before she gets the letter and another week or so before she responds. Then we will talk again. Since Kene left, it has left quite a gap in our lives. Ireland will be great for you, but I know it will take time for me to adjust to a new country other than America."

BACK IN IRELAND

Colleen went to the mailbox in the summer of 1960 and found Charlie's letter. A smile lit up her face as she read the words written on the paper. It was Saturday evening. She had just come home from working at the shop. She ran to the house and read the letter to Patrick. He was pleased to read that Charlie and family wanted to move to Donegal. He knew how much Colleen missed her son. This would be an answer to prayer for her. Her face glowed with happiness as she and Pat discussed this new turn of events. They talked for a while and decided it would be best for Charlie to move in with them. Pat needed help on the farm because he was spending so much time helping Colleen with her business. Pat decided to go see the local lumber company about plans for an addition.

The next day, he brought home some addition plans for the farm. It included three more rooms and another bathroom. Plumbing had come to Ireland in the late 1940s and they would put this bathroom close to the other one to share the same septic tank. With another family, a new tank would be the way to go.

Colleen studied the plan for a while and asked how much it would cost. Pat said he didn't know but would find out.

During the next few weeks, letters would be sent back and forth across the ocean. Josie and Charlie scanned the plans for the addition to Colleen's house. They finally agreed to one particular plan which had a staircase to two more rooms. They knew there would be additional children added to the family in the future.

They spent Thanksgiving and Christmas with just their little family in attendance. This would be the last of the holidays spent in Detroit. One evening in January, they discussed when they would be moving to Donegal.

Josie looked at Charlie with a smirk on her face. "No use asking you anymore when we would be moving to Donegal. I know, beyond a doubt it will be when the green grass grows!"

They both looked at each other and laughter rang across the living room. Charlie looked up at his dad's portrait. "Guess you will love moving to Ireland. You can hang up on my bedroom wall in Donegal."

They got out all of Colleen's notes on Ireland.

"Won't it be fun riding on the Jaunting Car, visiting the old castles, listening to Irish music and eating Irish stew and soda biscuits?" Charlie said and Josie agreed.

Along about March 31, they put up their home for sale. Several buyers went through it the next four weeks. Finally, on April 5, the real estate agent contacted them and told Charlie and Josie a black family wanted to move in.

Several others had bought homes in the neighborhood, and when the family came over to make final arrangements for the sale, they said they loved the house and would really feel at home here on the outskirts of Detroit. It was a neat, clean area, had excellent bussing, a wonderful school for their kids to attend and even a little church on Joy Road two blocks from 8254 Robson.

The new buyers would move in May 1, so the Stordahls could sell their furniture and any other belongings that they couldn't take with them. People from the Covenant Church came over first to pick out items they wanted.

Charlie went to the airport and bought tickets to Dublin, Ireland, where Colleen and Pat would pick them up on the last day in April. The green grass would be growing all over Michigan at that time. Spring was a beautiful time of the year. Josie's tulips and daffodils would be blooming. The robins would be back in the neighborhood building nests and getting ready to raise their little baby birds.

Colleen told them in her last letter that the grass seemed to take on a new particular shade of green, much lusher and softer to the feet than she could ever remember. She knew of Charlie's famous expression and recalled how he would stomp his right leg three times and leave to delve into a solution for his troublesome problems. This time, Charlie was more exuberant and joyful at the thought of the move to Donegal where the grass was greener and lusher than in Michigan.

The last day of April found them on the plane soaring up, up, up, and away to a new life with three precious children. The older ones looked forward to being with Grandmother

Colleen. They really loved her for she always had treats for them and lots of hugs and kisses.

The children behaved themselves quite well on the plane. Colleen told them stories and had color books for them to color in. They also took naps and had good meals on the plane as it flew over the ocean. They were up so high it was hard to see the land below. Most of the time was spent flying over the white clouds which the little ones found very delightful. Soon, the stewardess told them they were about to land at Dublin and to fasten their seat belts.

Little squeals of delight came from the older children. Baby Becky, who was a very good-natured baby, just took it all in and was very placid about the whole new venture in the lives of the Stordahls.

They made their way to the baggage claim area and waited for their bags to appear. They weren't there long when Colleen and Patrick arrived. The children squealed with excitement while hugging their grandma. They could hear laughter and excited people greeting each other while waiting for the luggage. After picking out their bags, Patrick led the way to the waiting car. It was a Ford Fairlane that he bought in Dublin two years ago. Charlie was glad to ride in the Ford. It reminded him of his childhood when his dad drove nothing but a Ford.

It was a three-hour ride to Donegal, but it went by fast. Tim and Debbie looked and looked out the window. They noticed all the farm lands. Each section was marked off with rows of stones and along each side of the road there were rows of stones. Cows and horses grazed in the fields. There were acres and acres of corn, potatoes, onions, and many other vegetable crops.

Charlie hoped and hoped with all his heart that they had made the right move. There would always be fond memories of growing up in Detroit and what a delightful childhood he had. He knew this would be different for his kids. Growing up on a farm, watching baby calves, pigs, and little chicks would sure be different than what he was accustomed to in Detroit.

When they drove up Pat and Colleen's driveway, they noticed tables and chairs were set up outside. Josie asked what was going on and Colleen told her that friends and neighbors and relatives had all been invited over to meet and greet her family from Michigan. They got out, took in all their belongings, inspected their new rooms, and just left most of the items on the bed and floor to be put away later on.

Around four in the afternoon, cars drove in and people came with pots and dishes of food and placed them and themselves around the table. Some brought Irish stew, some soda biscuits, some Irish chowder, salads, cake, and pie and other food items. They greeted the newcomers and introduced themselves and really made the Americans feel most welcome in the Irish Republic.

They had a wonderful time getting to know all these fine acquaintances of Colleen and Patrick. The party lasted until 8:00 that night. Charlie, Josie, and children were exhausted after all the clamor of the day. They tried their best to put away as much of their belongings as they could, but sleepiness came upon them and they decided to finish the next day.

Josie got up around 7:00 in the morning as sunlight streamed through the bedroom window. She looked over at Charlie, but he was still sound asleep. She joined Colleen and tried to help fix breakfast, but Colleen insisted that she sit back and drink some coffee and relax. Everything was under control. This was quite an undertaking as she and Patrick were used to having only the two of them to prepare meals for. She fixed oatmeal for the little ones and pancakes for the rest. Colleen didn't go to work that day. There was a lot to do yet to help the relatives from Detroit to get moved in and settled down.

That morning, they took Debbie and Tim out to look over the farm. They had never seen anyone milk cows before. They watched as the milk squirted into the pails. Debbie said, "I thought milk only came in bottles. I didn't know cows only ate grass and hay."

Patrick laughed and said, "Well, young 'un, your going to see a lot around here that you never saw in Detroit. I want to show you some little kittens that just opened their eyes. They are over here in this corner where mama kitty put her little family." Debbie and Tim each picked up a kitten and petted it while mama cat watched anxiously to make sure her kittens weren't injured. They played with the kittens quite awhile while Pat and Charlie milked the five cows. They sold some of the cream to stores in Donegal and made butter from the rest of the cream.

They covered every inch of the farm, looking at the new piglets and baby chicks. They also helped gather eggs and feed the chickens. Anyone could see how happy they were at Grandma's house.

20

Each day, there was something new to be discovered in Ireland. Colleen and Patrick took them around Ireland from time to time. Sometimes, they rode on the jaunting cars. Sometimes, they inspected the castles and ate supper there and were entertained by actors and actresses who put on special programs in the castles. They followed the way the River Shannon flows and went to Belfast, the main city in Ireland. It was something Josie had always dreamed of doing, and now those dreams came to pass.

By 1970, two more daughters had arrived in Donegal. There was Paula Marie and Lori May. Colleen's Bakery and Sewing Shop had been expanded. Debbie and Tim helped out, even though they were still children, at the bakery. There was a lot that they could do and they earned a little money that they could spend anyway that they wanted to.

Charlie continued to help Pat on the farm. Both he and Colleen were graying at the temples. Some arthritis had settled into Pat's legs and Colleen tired easily. Josie spent a few hours every day helping her out at the bakery. Colleen had taught her how to sew and read a pattern so she could help at the sewing room as well.

The family attended a little Lutheran Church in the city of Donegal. Debbie and Tim were confirmed there and they were brought up in the Sunday school.

They also had Sunday school picnics in Ireland and grade school outings. Charlie coached Tim's ball team the way his father used to coach him. The kids got bumps and bruises like normal kids. One day, Tim fell out of a tree, but he seemed to be all right. There were bad bruises on both legs for a week or two. He didn't much climb trees anymore looking for baby birds in their nest.

Debbie made friends with a little girl down the road and they played with their dolls together. Josie taught her how to sew on a treadle Singer sewing machine. Timmy had friends over that he played ball with. One of them was named Doug and they explored the fields and woods together. They were quite the mischief makers. One day, they put nails under Patrick's car tires, but Pat noticed it right away and Charlie gave him a good spanking and made him apologize. This hurt his dignity, but it also taught him a lesson he would never forget.

Little Becky played in a sandbox Pat had made for her and she was quite happy with her pails and shovels. She made houses and castles and loved playing by herself until some twins moved in down the road that were her age.

Pat built them a little doll house where they whiled away their time with dolls and tea parties.

Then the teenage years came for Debbie and Tim. The high school was two miles away so Charlie had to drive them there each day. They got to know many teenagers and attended basketball, baseball, football, and field hockey games. There were all kinds of classes to attend and they loved the school days in Donegal.

One day, Colleen put up her shop for sale. She was getting older and wanted to enjoy life away from working every day. It was three months before the shop was sold to Maureen and Mike Mac Namara. The family celebrated the sale by going camping in a tent on the shores of Galway Bay. They put up a tent and enjoyed the weekend camping, fishing, and hiking. It was fun to watch all the red curly-haired girls run up and down the beach. Wherever they went, people would look and smile at Charlie and Josie's girls. Tim looked rather out of place with his short-cropped blonde hair.

In the summer of 1971, Charlie, Tim, Debbie, and Patrick set out to bring the hay in from the fields. Pat had a small tractor which he used to till his garden, but for haying, he would hitch up the horses and they would pull a large wagon out on the field, and with pitchforks, the hay would be lifted in the wagon to take to the storage facilities in the barn. After taking in two loads of hay, they took their pitchforks and threw the final load of hay into the wagon. On the way back from the field, all were seated in the wagon while the horses trotted along. No need to tell them where to go, they knew the way by heart. All of a sudden, a little red fox ran across the two track road and the horses reared up into the air, and with a jolt, the wagon took off head long down the road. Heads bobbed up and down, hands gripped the sides of the wagon. Then the horses bolted from the road and the hay wagon went out of control. Pat and Charlie jumped from the wagon. Pat hit the ground with a thud and fell on his arm, which snapped in a severe break. Charlie ran after the horses and shouted at the horses, "Whoa whoa!"

The wagon careened head long ahead. Debbie was crying and Tim jerked the reins and yelled at the horses. He stood up and pulled as hard as he could on the reins. At last, the horses slowed down, and soon, Charlie caught up with them and stopped the runaways from going any farther.

Then Charlie and Tim ran back to tend to Pat's broken arm. Debbie was told to run to the house and tell Josie to get help bringing Pat to the hospital. Pat was held at the hospital because the arm had begun to swell. They kept him overnight to bring down the swelling so they could put a cast on the arm. What an afternoon that had been. It would be etched into the minds of those who had that experience and would never ever be forgotten.

21

Charlie and Josie continued to write to Kene and Trina in Atlanta, Georgia. Pictures of the children were sent to each other and their close bond continued to grow. Charlie related to them all the picturesque aspects of Ireland. Trina was especially interested in the scenic countryside and she would talk to Kene and tell him how wonderful it would be to move to Ireland and buy a farm close to Charlie's place.

Then long distance telephone calls were cheaper, so once a week, they would talk to each other on the phone. Josie was so glad to hear of Trina's interest in moving close to them. It sure would be wonderful to have them back into their lives.

Charlie and Josie began to look at farmhouses for sale. It seems in Ireland that one needed a document telling the future buyers that the land for sale was leprechaun free! Yes, it was fun each year to go on leprechaun hunts, but there was more involved than that. It seems that Irish people did not like the thought of leprechauns on their property. They were little tricksters and made life havoc with all their shenanigans. So in their hunt for a farm for Kene and Trina, they had to make sure that these little imps would not be a problem for them.

Charlie and Josie would laugh together about all the tricks that were played on different farms, supposedly, and make life hard for those farmers. Why, those little leprechauns would continually make it hard for people to sell land.

Maybe a leprechaun had scared the red fox that ran across the road that day out in the hay field. Whenever anything unexplainable happened, it was the leprechauns that were to blame.

One day about three miles from their farm, another farm went up for sale and it was declared leprechaun free. Josie sent Trina a picture of the house and told all the details of the farm, how many buildings there were, and how many outbuildings including the barn. It really did seem like a wonderful investment for the Carvers in Atlanta, Georgia.

When the envelope arrived at Trina's, she ripped it open with great delight and she scanned the picture for a long time, taking in all the details.

Trina could hardly wait until Kene came home from work. He, too, looked excitedly at the picture and read all the details of the outbuildings. There was no decision made for over a week when another letter came from Josie telling them that other buyers were interested, but so far, none of them had come up with the money. Trina wrote back that they would put their house up for sale, but there was no telling when that would happen or how long it would take, and so the waiting began.

Up went the for sale sign on their home. They did have some savings at the bank because Kene made excellent wages. The farm in Ireland was selling for $20,000 dollars. They knew they could sell their house for that amount and the savings account could go toward the farm in Ireland.

It was six months before the house sold, and when they had the money in the bank, they made a blank check out for the amount and mailed it to Josie in Donegal.

In the spring of 1973, when the green grass grows, the Carvers arrived at the airport in Dublin where Charlie and Josie met them at the baggage claim area. They would surely be good company for Debbie and Tim. They arrived in Donegal at 5:00 that evening and headed for the Stordahl home. What a grand time they had eating and reminiscing about times gone by. It was so good to be back together. They had really missed one another's company.

Later in the evening, young Kene Jr. came up to Charlie and said, "Mr. Charlie, what's all this talk about leprechauns?

Josie and I are really interested in learning all about these little critters that seem to be a nuisance here in Ireland."

Charlie looked at Kene Jr. with a twinkle in his eyes and a big grin on his face. "Well now, young man, leprechauns are quite intriguing. They spend a lot of time making shoes and store all their coins in a hidden pot at the end of the rainbow. If ever captured by a human, the leprechaun has the magical power to grant three wishes in exchange for their freedom."

Suddenly, Josie appeared and wanted in on the conversation. She sat down next to Charlie and lifted up her inquisitive face to hear more about the imps.

Charlie continued, "They are no taller than a small child with a beard and hat, although they may originally have been perceived as the tallest of the mound dwellers. I don't know much about mound dwellers. I haven't studied up on them. The leprechauns appeared in the medieval tale known as the Echtra Fergus Mac. The tale contains an episode in which Fergus Mac-leti, King of Ulster falls asleep on the beach and awakens to find himself being dragged into the sea by three Luchopain. He captures his abductors who grant him three wishes in exchange for his release and so this special ability now belongs to the leprechauns. He is a solitary creature who mends shoes and enjoys practical jokes (William Butler Yeats). They are not wholly good or wholly evil. Some dress in red or green depending upon which part of Ireland you live in. Their hats resemble the kind that Santa Claus wears. Each outfit is richly laced with gold, a cocked hat, shoes and buckles. Each jacket has seven rows of buttons. You might pass one on the road and never ever see it. They are really good at hiding. That's why it is hard to have your land free of the creatures. You have to really comb every part of the property to keep free of leprechauns. The Irish Poet William Allingham describes their appearance: a wrinkled, wizen'd, and bearded elf. Spectacles on his nose, a silver buckle on his hose, leather apron, shoe in his lap. You know, kids, this elf is very similar to the Swedish Tomtes. They are little elves or trolls that live under the houses and barns in Sweden. They bring good luck to those who dwell there and around Christmas time, they bring gifts for all the good boys and girls who live there."

Little Josie looked at Charlie and spoke in awe, "Wow, seems like every country has their share of these little creatures."

***A lot of these explanations of leprechauns come from Wikipedia, the free encyclopedia on the Internet.

22

The days that summer were filled with taking the children on hay rides, picnics, camping expeditions, fishing, and exploring the woods and forests. All took part in doing chores and helping around the farms of each other.

In July, little Lori was dressed in a traditional leprechaun outfit that Colleen had made. It was much like the outfit that was described by Charlie when telling them the stories of the leprechauns. The older children helped hide and protect Lori until the hunters came through looking for leprechauns. Only one young couple succeeded in capturing her from a well-hidden hiding place. Lori made the headlines in the paper the next day as the one that eluded capture the most with only one couple finding her. She received a $25 check that her parents deposited at the bank for her future education.

The time came for the older children to take driving courses so they could help with transporting younger children to camp, ball games, and other outdoor activities. Only one of the young people had a driving problem when little Josie stepped on the gas pedal instead of the brake and went crashing through the side of the garage. Of course, tears were shed and extra driving precautions were taken to make sure it wouldn't happen again.

One day, Debbie had a car load of young people and so did Kene Junior. They passed each other on the road and then decided to have a race to the next town. Speeds up to 100 miles an hour took place and the young people squealed with delight until Debbie hit a bump in the road and the car went airborne temporarily then crashed down. Everyone got a little scared and yelled for the driver to slow down. Well, Debbie did slow down and turned around and went back home with Kene Junior declared the winner. They never ever tried to do that again. It's a good thing the parents never found out about it until years later.

In 1980, Colleen had a major heart attack and died in her sleep on June 2. She was laid to rest and all the town mourned her passing. She was such an inspiration to all the townfolk. They gathered at the town hall afterward where the local church had a luncheon for all those who attended. There were many that spoke well of Colleen and all her accomplishments.

Charlie and Josie went to the courthouse and had their names placed upon the deed to the house that Colleen left to her son and his family

The years for the Carvers and Stordahls passed quickly. Kene Carver Jr. moved back to Detroit where he was employed at the Mardigan Plant as business manager. He met a very wonderful coworker that he married and gave Kene and Trina their first grandchild. Josie was employed in Donegal as a registered nurse after several years of study.

Tim, Debbie, and Becky Stordahl also moved back to one of the suburbs of Detroit. They studied at Michigan State University before making their homes in West Bloomfield Hills. They met their spouses at the Covenant Church. They also had grandchildren for Josie and Charlie.

They would write and tell their parents of the conditions of Detroit.

"The war on blight has spread beyond Detroit into Hamtramck and Highland Park. The two cities surrounded by Detroit are undertaking their first comprehensive attempts to count the number of blighted properties within their boundaries. Both municipalities have lost tens of thousands of residents and are packed with burned-out homes and abandoned buildings. Empty structures became havens for crime and squatters following the examples of what happened to the Detroit area. As a result, property values have plummeted."

This awful news was very alarming to Charlie and Josie who grew up in Detroit when it was at its zenith. They never thought this would happen to their beloved home city where they grew up. Henry Ford built his first auto plant there, and it soon became the Motor City Capital of the world. How sad!

It was once known as the city of trees. Elm trees bedecked every city for miles. Now blight came upon the trees and many were cut down and replanted with other species. The Model T plant has become another empty building that once employed many workers and put bread and butter on their tables.

Charlie said to Josie, "Lets not remember the way Detroit is today. Let's remember the way it used to be."

The years slipped away. Charlie and Josie were aging. Their hair was turning gray. Their bodies were slightly stooped. Arthritis was taking its toll on Josie. They had lived full and rich lives. They were pleased with the way their children had grown up to be. Christian, caring, loving, and living their lives as a blessing to all they met and had come into contact with at church. The farm no longer housed chickens, pigs, cows, and horses. Now just a milk cow and ten chickens for eggs were housed in the outbuildings. They planted a small garden each year and kept busy volunteering at nursing homes and church.

One day, early in the morning in the year 1998, Charlie stood in front of the fireplace, looking up at his father's picture above the mantle. He loved talking to his father, just as if he was alive and in the same room with him. He talked of Detroit and all that was going on there. "Do you remember, Dad, when you told me about the first car that the White House officials drove? It was a 1909 black car built by Ivan White and was known as the White Steamer. I also remember you telling me of the first drive-in gas station that you happened to go to in Pittsburgh in 1913?"

He continued, "Well, Dad, you might be interested to know that the first Corvette was white. This was unusual because for a long time all the cars built were black. Ford's answer to the Corvette was the 1960's Mustang, and the first car with a replaceable filter was the 1924 Chrysler. Dad, the first three-color traffic light was in Detroit in 1919. You probably went through it a few times on Woodward Avenue. The first car that used a key to get started was the 1949 Chrysler. The 1962 Chevy Impala was the first to go from 0-60 miles an hour in 60 seconds. You probably know all these facts, but then, you might be having such a good time in heaven that all these facts are quite trite and boring, but anyway, I thought I would talk to you this morning about these things 'cause I couldn't sleep and wanted someone to talk to. So here we go, Dad, more facts concerning cars in the Motor City. The lowest priced mass-produced car was the Ford Model T. That's the one you drove for several years. It was the 1925 Runabout and cost $260. There were lots of praises for the Ford V8. It was one of the finest cars of that time. Then there was the 1935

Jaguar and was known as a swallow side car. Ford was the first to make a pickup truck. They were shipped in crates as the beds of trucks. The new owners had to go to the dealers to get them, thus they were known as pickups. The trucks now are called Ford pickups. Well, Dad, I best be getting dressed and go out and milk those cows. Nice chatting with you."

So Charlie left to go out and do his chores. His face was lined with a few wrinkles here and there, but he was still a pretty handsome man. Josie also showed many signs of aging. She had grown quite plump, but was still outgoing and never lost her sense of humor. They were both well-pleased with living in Donegal. They were well-liked and always available to help out wherever they could to be good neighbors.

In the year 1998, Josie passed away. She had died in her sleep. The doctor said she just died of old age. She seemed to be in good health until then. Charlie was glad she hadn't suffered. All the children came to her funeral. She had died when the green grass grows in the spring and was laid to rest in the beautiful lush green cemetery in Donegal. Ireland truly was the land of the most beautiful green grass in the world.

Charlie passed just after the year 2000 was ushered in when the green grass grows in Donegal, May 15. He was found out in the barn tending the cows.

An autopsy was never performed. The family just accepted the fact that he truly missed his beloved Josie and had gone go be with her.

With the passing of their parents, the children were now orphans and no longer could confide in their beloved parents that had faithfully raised them to become what they were today. Their way of life and wisdom would always be there to guide them through major decisions that were made along life's pathway. Paula and Lori would inherit their house but would pay a share of the wealth with their siblings who lived in Michigan.

So we say good-bye to Charlie. His story will be an inspiration to all who read about his eventful, fulfilling life and what a blessing he was wherever he lived and to all who read his story.

POSTSCRIPT

I n the year 2012, Detroit filed for bankruptcy. In 2014, ten thousand small businesses came to the city and established their edifices. Thanks to funding from the Kresage and Skillman foundations, a Detroit firm, Hamtramck and Highland Park, was being renovated. Many blighted homes and businesses were bulldozed in the Detroit area. Clean-up crews from volunteers went through neighborhoods and did their best to renovate those areas.

Many buildings that were still of use were taken over by construction companies and remodeled into attractive homes and businesses. So Detroit seems to be on the move to becoming a hometown that people could once again be proud of.

SHIRLEY BERGSTROM

When the Green Grass Grows is really about my life growing up in Detroit. My dad worked for the Ford Motor Company until he retired and moved to Cheboygan, Michigan. Charlie is really me and all the adventures and trials I faced growing up in the Motor City. Many of the events are true and really happened. I still am concerned about Detroit which was at its Acme when I grew up there.

In 1952, I left Detroit and moved to Cheboygan where I raised my family. My children are Debbie Wiley, Timothy Bergstrom, Rebecca Reynolds, Paula Grawey, and Lori Leavitt.

I hope you will enjoy reading this book as much as I have writing it. I believe in Detroit and hope and pray it will once again be the Detroit that I remember.